Between Duty and Desire

Maryse Dawson

Published by Maryse Dawson, 2024.

Also by Maryse Dawson

Pirates Quest
Tides of Desire (Pirates Quest Book 1)
The Pirates Quest Collection
Captive to the Heart

Standalone
Taming the Willful Miss Roberts
Between Duty and Desire
Scandal in Silk: A Victorian Love Affair
Lily's Christmas Promise
A Passion for Annie
One Dreamy Knight

Watch for more at https://www.facebook.com/maryse.dawson.5.

Chapter 1

Lady Angelina Beaumont gazed out the window of her family's carriage as the sprawling manor house came into view. Even through the light rain pelting the glass, she could see the imposing stone facade and manicured lawns that spoke of Lord Sinclair's immense wealth and status.

Angelina closed her eyes and sighed, dreading what awaited her within those walls. She had argued until she was hoarse to try and wriggle out of this predicament but her father had refused to listen to her.

After the scandal of being caught alone with a stable boy at her Aunt's spring ball, her father had hastily arranged for her to come under the guardianship of his old friend, Lord Sebastian Sinclair. Lord Sinclair was a respected but stern man, and Angelina knew he wouldn't tolerate any impropriety from his new ward.

Her father was under the illusion that Lord Sinclair would be able to teach her how to behave as becomes a lady of her standing. It was all so silly! Of course she knew how to behave. She could embroider, speak French, play the piano, why, she could even sing if the occasion warranted it.

And now she was being sent here just because of one tiny indiscretion!

She had only met Lord Sinclair a couple of times and on both occasions, he'd been very intimidating. A man she wouldn't want to cross swords with yet here she was being packed off to his estate. She crossed her arms over her chest and sighed loudly.

The carriage rolled to a stop and Angelina steeled herself as she waited for the footman to open the door. Stepping outside, she lifted her skirts and darted through the rain towards the shelter of the manor's entrance. The big polished oak door was quickly opened and she was greeted by a stern-faced butler, "Good afternoon, Lady Angelina, I presume?"

Angelina nodded, and the butler stepped aside to let her into the large entrance hall. The footmen quickly arrived with her luggage, their gloved hands carefully carrying the ornate trunks and elegant hat boxes. They arranged the luggage in a neat row beside her, ensuring each piece was positioned just so. Angelina surveyed her belongings. She knew that her stay in this grand estate would be for quite a few weeks and had packed accordingly. Her maid, under her guidance, had packed her clothes very well.

As the butler closed the door behind her, she looked around, taking in the grandeur around her. Everything was decorated to a very high standard but her admiration turned to nervousness when the butler informed her that Lord Sinclair awaited her in his study.

Good lord, the moment had arrived. Taking a deep breath and steeling herself, she followed the butler along the hallway where he showed her into the wood-paneled study. There, standing rigidly beside the fireplace, was Lord Sinclair. His air of authority was unmistakable.

"Lady Angelina, welcome to Withdean. I trust your journey was comfortable?" he said in a deep, commanding voice. Angelina nodded politely and stared back at him, now up close she could study his features.

He was a very good looking man with short dark brown wavy hair and deep brown eyes that seemed almost black in the dim light of the room. He was only thirty-four but had the demeanor of someone much older. A certain poise and air of authority that people naturally respected. He was also very tall which made him appear even more intimidating.

But Angelina was no milksop and, as much as she felt unnerved by Lord Sinclair, he was soon going to find out that taming her was not going to be easy!

Lord Sinclair observed his new ward properly for the first time. Although he had seen her briefly before because of his connections with her father, he had never had the occasion to talk with her.

And now here she was, standing before him.

And what a beauty she was. In fact, she was exceptionally pretty and carried herself with a certain proud grace. Her long blonde hair was neatly pinned up in an attractive bun but it was her striking blue eyes he noticed most. Not only for their colour but the noticeable hint of rebellion within.

He took note of her fine features and lush figure, which no doubt contributed to the scandalous behaviour that had landed her in his care.

Beyond her beauty however, Lord Sinclair detected an unexpected spark of spirit and defiance within their depths. This was no meek, obedient lady accustomed to simpering at the whims of men. There was an independence, a devilment even, lurking behind her polite facade.

It was that spark that most concerned him and he now understood fully why her father had chosen to send her to him. For if left unchecked, such a willful nature could lead her down a path of ruin. But perhaps, properly guided and disciplined, that same fire could be transformed into a strength of character befitting her station.

I n that moment, Lord Sinclair understood the challenge before him - to rein in Angelina's wilder impulses, while nurturing the qualities that might serve her well as a lady of society and breeding. It seemed the task of taming this girl would be more intriguing than he had anticipated.

He decided to meet her rebellious temperament head on and said in a clipped, authoritative tone, "You will dine with me each evening promptly at seven o'clock. Lessons with your governess will take place each morning. Outside of scheduled activities, I expect you to occupy yourself in a manner befitting a lady of your station."

He watched her shrewdly, waiting to see if she would retaliate.

A ngelina felt her rebellious spirit rising at his domineering manner. "I am to have a governess?"

He nodded.

"But I don't need a governess! I am twenty-one years old. A-A governess is for children!"

"May I remind you, Lady Angelina, that you are here to learn about responsibility and manners befitting your station." He fixed her with a hard stare, "Or had you forgotten?"

Angelina felt her temper begin to rise and even though she knew it wouldn't do to challenge him so directly, she couldn't help herself, "I want to leave."

He quirked an eyebrow and shook his head, "I am afraid you cannot."

Angelina balled her fists at her sides, "You intend to keep me prisoner?" Her eyes flashed fire.

Lord Sinclair moved over to her and taking her small chin in his, he forced her to look up at him. His eyes were dark and commanding, making her catch her breath. "I can see very well now why your father sent you here. You are far too undisciplined and headstrong. But I intend to change that."

Angelina felt her cheeks burning under Lord Sinclair's piercing gaze. Before she could gather her wits to respond, he walked to the door. "Wilson?"

At Lord Sinclair's call, his butler materialized promptly in the hallway. "Yes, my lord?"

"Please show Lady Angelina to her chambers. She appears a little fatigued from her journey."

Although his words were polite, Angelina knew he was dismissing her. He turned his back, effectively ending their conversation.

Angelina thought about arguing back but had no desire to make a scene in front of Wilson. So huffing loudly to let Lord Sinclair hear her vexation, she followed the butler out into the hallway.

Wilson led her up the grand staircase and down a hallway lined with portraits of Lord Sinclair's aristocratic ancestors. Their eyes seemed to follow her, judgmental and accusing.

At the end of the hall, Wilson gestured to an ornate set of double doors. "These will be your chambers, my lady, for the duration of your guardianship," he stated politely. "The maids will attend to any needs you may have."

Stepping inside, Angelina, despite her simmering temper, gasped softly at the luxurious furnishings. A four-poster bed draped in silks, a plush sitting area, and a private balcony overlooking the gardens. It was very opulent but extremely inviting.

The maids had just finished unpacking her trunks and were smoothing the folds of her dresses in the wardrobe.

"Hurry along you two!" Wilson waved his finger at them. Angelina saw one of them flash him an exasperated look and in that moment, realised she may have met someone she might be able to make friends with. It lifted her spirits instantly.

"Shall I arrange for some tea to be brought up, my lady?" Wilson asked her.

"Oh, yes, that would be lovely."

When he had gone, Angelina took a moment to admire the view from the balcony, it looked over the beautiful lawns and gardens. She hoped she would be able to wander freely amongst them but if not, perhaps there was a way of using the balcony to her advantage without Lord Sinclair's knowledge. She had often climbed trees as a child and in all truth, still did on occasion. So scaling a balcony should be no problem. She smiled wickedly. Oh yes, he might think he had the upper hand, but he truly didn't!

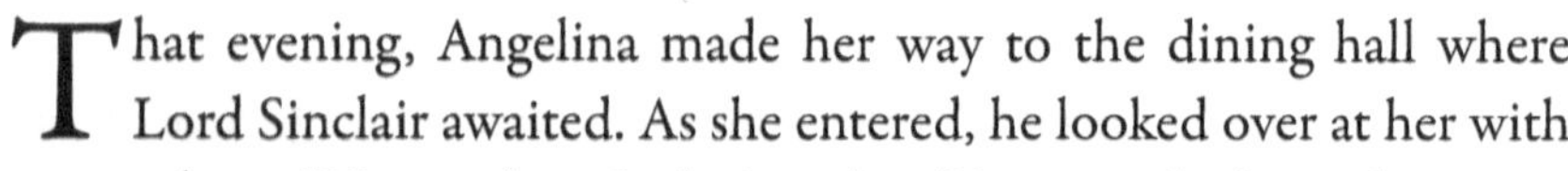

That evening, Angelina made her way to the dining hall where Lord Sinclair awaited. As she entered, he looked over at her with a critical eye. "You are late, Lady Angelina," he remarked sternly.

She slid into the seat that Wilson held out for her, "Forgive me, my lord. I was detained." She hadn't been. She just wanted to annoy him so she had dithered over which dress to wear, ensuring she would be ten minutes late. She kept her lashes lowered to hide her satisfaction.

Lord Sinclair merely hummed in response, signaling for the first course to be served.

As they ate the first course of soup with warm bread rolls, Lord Sinclair asked her about her home life. "You have one brother and one sister, do you not? Yet neither are as undisciplined as you. Perhaps it's because you are the youngest. I think perhaps your parents have been too lenient, but we can change all that."

Angelina's fiery spirit began to rise within her once more. Deliberately, she leaned her chin upon one delicate hand, her elbow poised unforgivingly on the table. Lord Sinclair eyed her with disapproval.

"Mind your manners, Lady Angelina. A lady sits with poise and decorum at all times."

His chiding only served to further her defiance. "Must you be so formal, my lord? We are the only two present, what does it matter?"

Lord Sinclair's eyes flashed with warning. "In this house, you will conduct yourself properly. That's the main reason you are here."

Angelina opened her mouth for a sharp retort, but Lord Sinclair silenced her with a stern look. "That's quite enough. You are beginning to try my patience! I suggest you think on how to reform your wild ways, lest you find yourself with less favourable circumstances."

With that, he returned resolutely to his meal. But Angelina was not so easily subdued. "What do you mean by *less favourable circumstances*?"

"It means, my lady, that I will have no hesitation in turning you over my knee or over the end of your bed and giving you a good hiding."

Angela gasped, "How dare you say such a thing!"

He raised his finger and pointed at her in warning, "If you carry on in this vein, you will leave me no choice but to spank your bottom because one way or another, you *will* learn to behave!"

She lowered her eyes, cheeks flushing. But beneath the table, her fingers curled into a defiant fist. This man might be her guardian, but she had no intention of being so easily tamed. How dare he threaten to spank her! Her of all people!

Unable to stop herself, she retorted rudely, "I think your attitude is uncalled for!" Her bottom lip pouted with indignation.

"And yours leaves a lot to be desired." He tapped his fingers on the table, "If you don't want a spanking, then you will behave as befits a lady. It is that simple."

"My father would never have sent me here if he knew what you intended." She eyed him sulkily.

His eyes met hers. "Your father gave me leave to discipline you as I feel fit and I, my dear Lady Angelina, believe that a good old fashioned spanking can cure many an ailment, including a precocious nature. So, if you wish to avoid such punishment, you had better learn to curb your tongue and do as you're told."

She pursed her lips and cursed him silently, knowing that if she said it out loud, then her backside would take the brunt.

They ate the rest of the dinner in silence. It should have been a really delicious meal but it all tasted like sawdust to Angelina. She was too busy lamenting the fact she was even there and that she now found herself in the hands of a tyrant.

After the tense dinner, Lord Sinclair informed Angelina she was dismissed to retire for the evening.

"You will meet me in the music room at nine o'clock sharp. If you are late, it will be noted."

With a brief, dismissive nod he left her standing in the dining room, wondering how on earth she was going to get out of her predicament. One way or another, she had to leave.

The next morning, Lady Angelina found herself in the music room after breaking her fast. She had thought about arriving late and then remembered his warning. Was he just bluffing? Would he actually carry out such a threat? Her buttocks clenched at the mere thought of such a punishment. He had certainly seemed sincere.

She didn't know him well enough yet to know how much she could play him, so erring on caution she chose to actually be there on time and avoid a reprimand.

There, seated at a gleaming grand piano, was Lord Sinclair awaiting her arrival.

"Good morning, Lady Angelina. I trust you slept well?" He turned his head to look at her, his dark eyes penetrating hers. He looked more handsome than ever.

He was dressed in a well-tailored dark grey suit with a crisp white cravat accentuating his strong jaw, looking every inch the aristocratic gentleman.

Angelina felt a flutter in her chest at the sight of him, his lean muscles evident even beneath layers of fine fabric. Though she knew it was most inappropriate, she couldn't deny a certain physical attraction had begun to form.

Chastising herself for such wayward thoughts, she strode into the room as gracefully as she could muster and answered his question, "Yes, thank you. The bed was most comfortable."

"Excellent. Now, come and sit beside me. You will take a lesson from me every morning," he announced in a no-nonsense tone. "A lady of quality must be well-versed in the arts."

Angelina bit back a retort, seating herself obediently on the piano bench beside him.

"Can you play the piano?" he asked, his deep voice reverberating around the room.

Angelina nodded, feeling a little unsettled at being in such close proximity to him. He seemed larger than ever.

She watched him flick open the pages of a music book and choosing a song sheet, he told her to begin.

She placed her fingers on the keys and began to play the tune. She wasn't brilliant but in all fairness she wasn't bad. Although what Lord Sinclair would think, only time would tell.

A few moments later, she heard him tut out loud. Good lord, even her piano playing wasn't good enough!

He began instructing her in scales and the correct way to position her hands. She soon found her mind wandering. This was only her first day and she was already finding it terribly annoying. She glanced out of the window, wishing she was riding out across the fields.

Seeing her distraction, Lord Sinclair's voice took on a stern edge. "Pay attention, Lady Angelina. Posture straight, fingers curved as so." He adjusted her hands himself, sending an unexpected spark through her at his touch.

Now even more flustered, Angelina stumbled over the keys. Lord Sinclair sighed in frustration. "Again. And this time, focus if you please."

She tried, but the fiery look in his eyes as he watched her only served to fluster her further. When her hands slipped yet again, Sinclair grasped them firmly to demonstrate the proper form. The feel of his strong fingers over hers was most disconcerting, and quite against her will, Angelina felt her cheeks flush pink.

"You seem distracted, Lady Angelina," Sinclair remarked. "Are you like this at home or is it just for my pleasure?"

She huffed, "No, I do very well at home. In fact, I think you should send me back now." She flung her hands out, "You can see that I can play the piano. I don't need any further lessons at all." She went to stand up and he pulled her back down.

"I am the one who will decide when you are ready to return home and believe me, you are a long way off. Now, please, continue the lesson."

Just as she was deciding whether or not to have a hissy fit and storm out of the room, a knock sounded at the music room door. Lord Sinclair straightened with a sigh. "Enter."

Wilson appeared, bowing respectfully. "Pardon the interruption, m'lord, but a Miss Preston has arrived - she is the new governess you were expecting."

Lord Sinclair nodded briskly. "Show her in." He turned to Angelina, voice stern. "We will continue afterwards. Do try to apply the corrections."

Angelina bit back a retort as the newcomer was shown inside. Miss Preston curtsied gracefully, surveying the scene with interest behind wire-rimmed spectacles.

"Miss Preston, this is Lady Angelina," said Lord Sinclair by way of introduction. "You will oversee her education and deportment henceforth."

Angelina frowned - another tyrant to restrain her spirit! She regarded the woman with keen eyes, trying to assess if she was friend or foe. She looked very prim and proper and was older than her by about ten years or so.

Miss Preston pressed her lips into a thin line as she took in Angelina's posture at the piano. "Well, I can see we shall have to start with your posture, my lady." Her voice was crisp and no-nonsense. "It leaves a lot to be desired, I can tell you."

Angelina bristled. Yes, she was most definitely foe.

Lord Sinclair nodded, obviously in agreement and turning to Angelina, said. "I think we will finish the piano lessons for today. I will leave you under Miss Preston's instruction for the rest of the morning. It will give you time to get to know one another properly."

Angelina looked over at the governess. Her gaze was steely through her spectacles and she said brusquely. "I would like to start with your comportment. Let me see you walk across the room."

Angelina rose and began to awkwardly walk across the music room. She was too keyed up to put on an act and her frustration at finding herself in such a situation was a little overwhelming.

Miss Preston tutted disapprovingly. "Just as I suspected. No good at all. Well then, we shall start with posture and carriage immediately."

It seemed Angelina's rebellious spirit had met its match in the stern Miss Preston. She sighed inwardly, how was she going to fare under such a formidable new teacher? And more to the point, how the hell was she going to escape?

Chapter 2

After a light lunch, which she chose to take in her room, Angelina lay on the bed and stared up at the ceiling.

Miss Preston had proved to be a complete harridan and it had taken all of Angelina's strength to refrain from giving her a mouthful. But if she did, she knew the governess would go straight to Lord Sinclair and she'd be in all sorts of trouble. Oh lord!

She bashed the pillow next to her angrily. How long must she suffer this horrendous situation?

Amy bustled into her room, a smile on her face. "I've just come to take your tray, m'lady."

Angelina smiled back and sat up. Amy was the maid she had encountered yesterday and had taken an instant shine to. She was a happy soul and about the same age. Patting the bed, Angelina told her to take a seat.

"I can't be too long, m'lady." Amy said, "The cook will be on my case if I don't get back soon."

"Oh, tell her I needed you to help me change outfits or something." Angelina suggested. "She'll never know."

Amy giggled and sat down on the soft mattress, quickly asking, "How are you finding it here at Withdean, m'lady?"

Angelina rolled her eyes. "Extremely tiresome! Lord Sinclair thinks he owns me, and the new governess is devoid of humour!"

Amy pulled a face, "Oh dear! I saw her earlier, she took lunch with us in the kitchens and she seems very straight-laced I must say. She didn't laugh at anything Bertie had to say. He's one of the footmen and can be very amusing." She looked down at the coverlet. "Obviously not to Miss Preston though."

"I think her face might crack if she smiled." Angelina laughed.

Amy sniggered and then asked, "Do you have to have lessons every day?"

Angelina nodded. "Lucky me, eh?"

She saw a sly look cross Amy's face and immediately leaned forward, asking, "What is it? What have you thought of?"

Amy glanced over her shoulder and then whispered, "You could always be ill tomorrow? At least have one day's break from routine."

Angelina's eyes widened. "What a wonderful idea!" She thought hard, "I could pretend to be slightly unwell at dinner and that will make it more realistic when I pronounce that I am sick in the morning." She grabbed Amy's hand. "Will you help me?"

"Of course!"

That evening, as Lady Angelina entered the dining hall, Lord Sinclair found himself observing her more closely than intended. She wore a gown of pale blue silk that accentuated her hourglass figure and brought out the shine of her blonde hair, done up neatly yet allowing a few wisps to frame her face.

At once poised and radiant, she looked every bit the English rose. Lord Sinclair pondered that with proper guidance and seasoning, Angelina could make a match beneficial to any lord.

And yet, the thought caused an unsettling twist in his gut. To picture this beautiful woman bound to the will of another man sparked an unexpected feeling of jealousy.

He took a steadying sip of wine. She had been under his care for not even two days and yet already she was getting under his skin, one way or another. He dismissed his jealous thoughts and willed himself to have some self discipline. His ward was here to learn from his experience and his standing in society and he would damn well push any feelings he may have to the side.

Miss Preston's arrival today seemed to have already made changes that were clearly evident. Angelina moved with newfound grace and poise to her seat. She inclined her head politely to him in greeting, hands folded neatly in her lap as they began their meal.

"I see Miss Preston has made progress with you," he remarked.

"Yes, my lord. She has been very thorough in my instruction."

Lord Sinclair detected a hint of strain beneath Angelina's polite tone. "And do you find her methods effective, my lady?"

Angelina paused, choosing her words carefully. "She is a little strict but as you have told me, I am here to learn so it must be in my best interests."

He narrowed his eyes a little. Although she spoke the words, he could tell that beneath them there was insincerity. But it was early days, at least she was trying.

Angelina's fiery spirit was not going to be easily tamed.

As they ate, a comfortable silence fell. She even asked him about his day. Which later, he would reflect upon and wonder why he hadn't seen the warning signs but hindsight was a wonderful thing.

For now, he found himself caught up in the flow of conversation. She proved to be an attentive listener and the evening soon became nightfall. With a warning not to be late for her lessons in the morning, Lord Sinclair bid her good night.

The next morning, as Angelina stretched her slender legs beneath the coverlet, there came a knock at her bedroom door. Amy entered, curtsying with a sly smile.

"Good morning, m'lady. I've brought you some hot water for your ablutions." She peered at her intently and said, "Though you seem a bit peaky if you ask me." Amy eyed her mistress knowingly.

Angelina quickly caught on, playing her part. "I confess I am feeling quite unwell. I wonder if it was something I ate yesterday. I fear my lessons will have to be missed today."

Amy clucked her tongue. "Oh dear, that is such a shame. I know how much you were looking forward to them." She smiled. "Now let me feel your brow." She placed her hand on Angelina's forehead and tutted loudly, "As I suspected, I think you have a fever. Best stay in bed and rest."

Angelina suppressed a giggle. Having someone to help her was a Godsend.

A little while later, there was a sharp knock on the door. Amy opened the door and Miss Preston breezed in. She walked straight over to Angelina and peered into her face, her eyes suspicious.

On Amy's advice, Angelina coughed pathetically into a handkerchief and then gave a little groan. "I am truly sorry, Miss Preston but I feel far too unwell to attend a lesson this morning."

The governess's stern gaze swept over her and laying a hand on Angelina's brow, said, "You don't seem very hot to me." She turned on Amy and said accusingly, "I thought you said she had a raging fever?"

Amy gulped and Angelina quickly came to her aid, "Oh, I was burning up earlier but Amy kindly applied some cold water to my face and although the heat has diminished I just don't feel well enough to get out of bed." She coughed again into the handkerchief for good effect.

Thankfully, it seemed to work. Miss Preston took a step back. "Very well. But you are to remain in bed all day, do you hear? And I will ask the cook to make you a clear broth. That is all you are allowed today. It will cleanse your system."

Angelina just managed to hide the look of horror that threatened to appear on her face. Just broth? All day? Good lord, she'd pass out with hunger. Her eyes darted to Amy's. Hopefully she would be able to bring her some proper food.

"I will come and sit with you later this morning. Perhaps I could read to you?" Miss Preston suggested.

Angelina's eyes widened and coughing again, she said weakly, "I think, if you don't mind, I will go to sleep. My mother always says a good sleep cures many an ailment."

Miss Preston raised an eyebrow, clearly not in agreement. "Very well. I will inform Lord Sinclair of the situation when he returns this afternoon."

She left without another word and Angelina sighed with relief, "Really sympathetic, isn't she? I wouldn't want to be truly ill under her watch! Goodness me." She looked at Amy, "Will you be able to bring me some food later. I can't survive on broth all day!"

Amy laughed, "Oh, fear not, m'lady, I'll snaffle some food and bring it up after lunch."

Left alone, Angelina lay in bed thinking about what Miss Preston had said: that Lord Sinclair was out.

This surely was a golden opportunity to escape, wasn't it? She could slip out of the manor, walk to the village and then hail a carriage for home. She chewed on her nail, thinking hard. But how would her father react when she turned up on the doorstep? He would only send her back here and then she'd be in even more trouble with both him and Lord Sinclair. Oh, my.

She thumped the coverlet angrily. If only she hadn't canoodled with Edward then she wouldn't even be here. It wasn't as though they had even kissed, he had just put his arms around her and that was that. Caught in the act and her life forever changed.

Mind you, so was his. She'd heard he had been dismissed from his post at Fenwick. She paused, wondering what he was doing now.

She'd bet he wasn't having to endure such rigid reforms as she was experiencing.

Amy slipped back into the room and rushed over. "I took this from the kitchens. It was right under Miss Preston's nose and she never saw a thing!" She laughed at her own cunning. "Eat it quickly in case the old hag decides to come back!"

Angelina's eyes lit up when she saw the freshly baked pastry and quickly took it from Amy, biting into the still warm delicacy. She closed her eyes with bliss. "Oh lord, that is so good!"

"I thought you'd appreciate it. I can bring you something else later as well."

"Oh, you are so thoughtful. I am so glad you are here. I don't think I could cope without you." And she meant it. An idea came to her and lowering her voice she asked, "Is there any way that I could go outside without anyone seeing? I mean to say, is there a side entrance that I could sneak out of? I would dearly love to have some fresh air."

In hushed tones, Amy explained that there was a side entrance to the gardens. "If you are quick, m'lady, you could slip out unseen. When you've eaten that pastry, I'll help you dress and then I'll go and see who's about before letting you know if it's safe or not."

Half an hour later and her heart racing with anticipation, Angelina donned a light shawl as she followed Amy out of the bedroom and down the stairs. If Miss Preston caught her she was going to be in so much trouble but her desire for the outdoors overcame any trepidation.

They had put pillows under the coverlet to make it seem like she was still in bed and Amy had promised to keep a look out for her. If anyone asked she would say that Angelina was still ill, if not worse and that she needed rest.

Staying close to the walls, the two women flitted silent as shadows down back stairways. At last they reached the side door, sunlight beckoning just beyond. Amy gave Angelina's hand a squeeze.

"Enjoy the brief freedom!"

With that, Angelina slipped into the gardens, feeling quite daring. She breathed the fresh air, reveling in this small taste of freedom and quickly headed towards the walled gardens.

Lord Sinclair returned to his estate after a long morning in town. As he stepped out of the carriage, a flash of color through the hedges caught his eye.

Curious, he veered toward the gardens, pushing aside the foliage. What he glimpsed stole his breath: Lady Angelina, alone amid the blossoms. Unaware of his gaze, she walked leisurely through the greenery, skirts swirling about her lithe form, her blonde tresses shining like gold in the dappled sunlight.

In that private, unguarded moment, Lord Sinclair saw past the willful little rebel to the young woman beneath. Her radiant joy was obvious and her stunning beauty outshone even the flowers in full bloom.

He knew he should announce his presence but a selfish impulse kept him hidden, craving a while longer to simply observe her innocent revelry undisturbed.

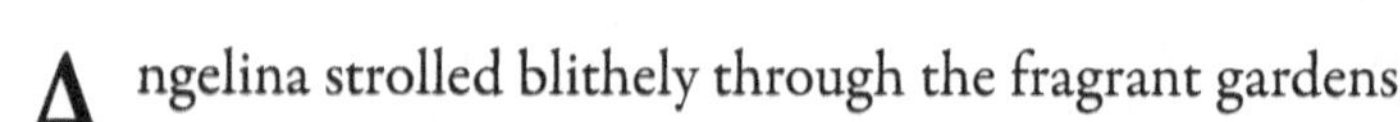

Angelina strolled blithely through the fragrant gardens, basking in the stolen moments of solitude. Away from the stern governess and her boring lessons, she walked carefree amidst the blooms, lifting her face to the warmth of the sun.

It was such a beautiful day and to be cooped up inside would be unbearable!

As she gazed upon a beautiful rosebush heavy with blooms, Angelina plucked a single blossom, lifting it to breathe its perfume. She smiled, thoroughly enjoying the chance to be her true self.

Blissfully unaware of Lord Sinclair's covert observance, Angelina continued her revels for a while longer before reluctantly heading back to the manor, the pretty rose grasped in her hand.

Once inside, she silently made her way up to her bedroom and slipped inside unnoticed. Putting her pillows back in place, she lay on the bed and grinned like a Cheshire cat. What a wonderful escape that had been!

It wasn't long before Amy arrived with a clear broth. Angelina wrinkled her nose at the sight of it and then brightened up perceptively when Amy produced a little plate of finely sliced beef. Grinning appreciatively, she dived into the delectable fare.

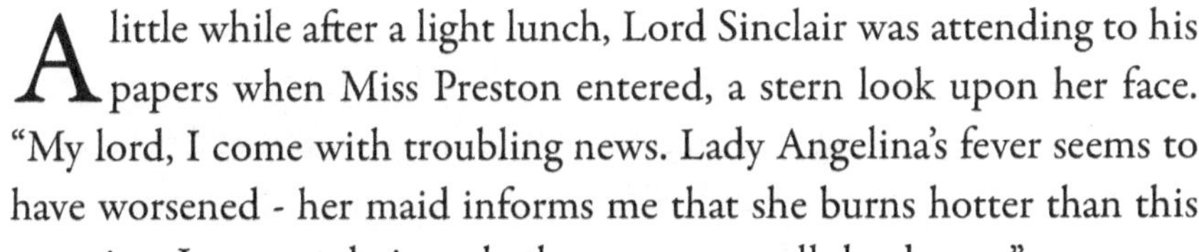

A little while after a light lunch, Lord Sinclair was attending to his papers when Miss Preston entered, a stern look upon her face. "My lord, I come with troubling news. Lady Angelina's fever seems to have worsened - her maid informs me that she burns hotter than this morning. I am wondering whether or not to call the doctor."

Lord Sinclair sat back in his chair and frowned. "She is ill, you say?"

Miss Preston nodded. "Indeed. She missed her lessons this morning due to her ill health. I fear she will be unable to attend your instruction this afternoon for the same reason."

He thought hard. Hadn't he seen Angelina dancing freely in the gardens mere hours ago? It was definitely her, of that there was no doubt and there had certainly been no hint of a fever from what he had witnessed.

Something was afoot and that little madam had some questions to answer.

Deciding to keep her misbehaviour to himself for the moment he spoke with authority to Miss Preston, "I see. Can you ensure she is attended to? Her comfort is a priority. I shall come along myself to inspect her condition presently and if I think it fitting, I will ask the doctor to call."

Miss Preston left and Lord Sinclair quietly perused the facts, quickly concluding that Lady Angelina had deliberately avoided her lessons. Well, she would soon learn that he wouldn't tolerate such behaviour.

When he arrived at Angelina's bedroom, Lord Sinclair threw open the door without preamble.

Instead of discovering a poorly girl confined to her bed due to a fever, he was greeted by the sight of a remarkably healthy lady, immersed in the pages of a book, radiating contentment.

"Lord Sinclair!" Angelina cried, color rising at being caught in her deceit. But Lord Sinclair's steely gaze stopped any excuse before it passed her lips.

"Do not trouble yourself with falsehoods - I am aware of your supposed illness being nothing but a ruse." His voice hardened as he continued, "To so brazenly flout your lessons and governess is unacceptable. You will face the consequences of these actions, Lady Angelina, have no doubt."

Chastised, Angelina dropped her gaze, cheeks flaming.

"Follow me down to my study. You and I are going to have a proper conversation."

Angelina's heart was thumping so hard in her chest she feared it would jump right out. She risked a glance at Lord Sinclair. He was sitting at his desk, opposite her with a face set in stone.

She licked her lips nervously and tried to pretend an air of innocence.

Lord Sinclair tapped the desk with his fingers and eyed her critically. "So, what do you have to say for yourself?"

Angelina opened her mouth to begin but Lord Sinclair held up a hand. "Before you even think of lying to me, know that I saw you in the gardens earlier and you were most definitely not ill."

She flushed under his piercing gaze. He continued, his voice low and commanding. "You are to be a credit to your station, not a willful, rebellious child. You will redouble your studies and submit to Miss Preston's authority without question. Is that clear?"

Angelina's eyes widened and she jumped up from her seat. "Double? That is unfair!"

"Do you dare argue with me?" He said, his eyes turning dark.

She caught her breath but was too het up to stop. "Yes!"

"Well then, I can see that I have only one option."

He stood up and walked around the desk towards her but she had already anticipated his move and quickly turned to run, evading his grasp. Fleet of foot, she sped towards the oak door, hoping to outrun him.

But she wasn't fast enough and soon felt a firm hand close around one of her wrists. "Let me go, my lord!" she squealed, struggling and pulling backwards, while slapping at his hand with her free one. "You have no right to manhandle me!"

He quickly moved her over to his chair and sitting down, he upended her straight over his solid thighs. "I gave you fair warning!"

She felt her skirts lifted and then a sharp sting as his hand laid into her bloomer-clad bottom. She gasped with shock and tried to push herself off him but his grip was too tight. His free hand walloped her backside with precise accuracy and all she could do was kick out and cry as each spank fell.

"How dare you!" she cried out.

"I dare, Lady Angelina. You are insolent and rebellious. But you will soon learn how to behave!"

"I hate you!" She grit her teeth as he continued to spank her, slapping her buttocks alternately, his hand feeling more like iron than flesh. How could he inflict so much pain with just his hand?

Finally, when her bottom was like a furnace, he let her up. She backed away from him, rubbing furiously at her posterior and looking at him with indignation.

"You had no right to do that!" she cried.

"I had every right! You are disobedient and wayward. The way you behaved today was abominable. Did you think it acceptable to act like that? Deceiving poor Miss Preston who is only here to try and teach you how to act with decorum as befits a lady of your station?"

Angelina scowled.

"And take that look off your face else I take the cane to your defiant little behind." He threatened.

Despite being annoyed at him, she found herself responding to his dominance, a frisson of excitement coursing through her. She wasn't sure why and didn't quite understand her feelings.

But she knew to obey him for he would surely carry out his threat. Reluctantly and taking a lot of effort, she managed to lower her eyes to hide her anger.

"Now, you will not only have lessons in the morning for the next few days but I will take it upon myself to personally instruct you in the afternoons. And if you dare so much as argue back I shall have no hesitation in spanking your bottom until you obey me. Do you understand?" His eyes bored into hers, brooking no disobedience.

Her eyes widened in alarm. The man was mean enough to do it again, she could see that.

"And the gardens are out of bounds until further notice!"

Thrusting out her bottom lip mulishly, she balled her fists at her side and nodded. She couldn't speak for fear of getting herself into trouble again.

Her fiery nature wanted nothing more than to tell him to go to hell but the consequences would mean a brush with the cane. Her bottom was tender enough as it was without a few strikes of that blasted thing!

So Angelina had no choice but to nod, chastened. As Lord Sinclair dismissed her sternly, she wondered how long she could endure such tight reins on her free spirit. Their battle of wills was surely not over.

Chapter 3

T*he next day*

Lady Angelina arose with a weary sigh, dreading the day ahead. After her scolding and spanking from Lord Sinclair, she knew Miss Preston would be twice as rigorous during lessons.

What a day that had turned out to be. Her bottom was still sore but she was thankful it had only been his hand she experienced. The mere thought of a cane made her clench her buttocks with dread. Good lord!

Last night she had dined alone in her chambers, Lord Sinclair having declared he wanted her to reflect upon her behaviour. To be honest after the way he had treated her, she had no desire to sit in embarrassed silence throughout a five course meal. Lord, she still couldn't believe he had spanked her.

Amy arrived to help her dress and revealed that Lord Sinclair had scolded her as well, for her part in the whole saga. He had, however, decided not to dismiss her and allow her another chance to prove herself worthy of her position.

Angelina sympathised with her and confided that Lord Sinclair had done the unthinkable and actually spanked her. Amy's jaw nearly dropped to the ground.

So together, they agreed to keep things above board and orderly... for now.

At breakfast, Angelina kept her eyes downcast, aware of Lord Sinclair's watchful gaze upon her. How she longed to run away but there was no help for it now. She had got herself into this predicament and only she could get out of it... by behaving. But could she do it?

As the clock struck nine, Angelina made her reluctant way to the parlour where Miss Preston awaited. The governess's hawk-like eyes immediately found fault. "You dawdled. Tardiness will not be tolerated."

Angelina bit her tongue, willing herself to remain composed. She knew that to endure this charade, she must play the part of a reformed lady convincingly. It was going to be damned hard though.

Seating herself primly at the desk, Angelina organised her writing instruments and folded her hands in her lap, gazing ahead with feigned attentiveness. Beneath her serene facade, schemes of rebellion simmered. But until a chance arose, she would grin and bear the boring lessons, nodding and reciting as expected.

She had every intention of making her performance flawless for the sooner she could leave, the better. The thought of having to endure another spanking, made her squirm uncomfortably on her seat. Something that Miss Preston immediately admonished her for.

"Don't fidget! Hold your back straight!"

Angelina sucked in a breath and did as she said, pressing her lips together tightly in order to contain the venomous words that were threatening to fall from her lips! Lord, it was so frustrating, the desire to snap at her was overwhelming.

"I see you are recovered from your malady." Miss Preston remarked, her eyes speculative. "At one point I thought we would have to call the doctor."

Angelina looked at her sharply. Had Lord Sinclair refrained from telling her the truth? It would seem so, for there was no admonishment forthcoming.

"No, I am much recovered today." she said, wondering why he hadn't told her. But she didn't have long to dwell upon it as Miss Preston was already starting her morning's lesson.

"Good, then we will begin. Today we shall study history." She turned her back and picked up a large book. Angelina pulled a face at her and poked out her tongue.

The morning wore on, and the histories grew more arduous. When she misspoke, Miss Preston slapped the desk in front of her sharply, making her jump.

By midday, Angelina's patience had worn thin. As the lesson dragged on, her mind wandered to the gardens beyond, now forbidden to her. How she ached to run wild and free once more.

At last her morning instruction came to a welcome end, and Angelina gathered her things eagerly. Walking sedately to the door under the watchful eyes of Miss Preston, she bid her good day and as soon as the door closed, she ran off in a flurry of skirts towards her own chambers.

She only had a brief respite before her afternoon's tutoring with Lord Sinclair and she was going to make the most of it! She had a feeling it was going to be a long day!

Reaching her rooms, Angelina collapsed onto her settee with an exhausted sigh. "I fear I shall die of boredom if I am forced to endure one more dreary lecture! I can't keep this up!"

Amy tutted sympathetically, laying out a light lunch. "The lessons do seem dreadfully dull, m'lady. Come and have a bite to eat. A good meal will lift your spirits."

Angelina angled her head to see what food Amy had served out and immediately perked up. There was a lovely variety. That was one positive thing she could say about Withdean Manor - the cook knew a thing or two about preparing meals.

Amy settled her mistress at the table and picked up the tray to leave. Angelina stopped her. "Can't you stay a while?" She picked up a dainty sandwich and held it out. "Share some of this with me. No one will know. Besides, there is far too much for me here."

A mischievous gleam appeared in Amy's eye. "I shouldn't really, m'lady but I haven't had lunch yet and I don't think anyone will miss me for a few minutes."

"Well, come on then." Angelina patted the chair next to her. "Just keep me company. I am dying to hear some gossip about Lord Sinclair."

Amy threw caution to the wind and sat down, taking the sandwich and biting into the tasty offering.

"So, tell me something about Lord Sinclair. Does he have a lady friend? A fiancée? What is his family like?"

"Well," Amy began, "He has a younger sister but we don't see her very often. Her name's Lady Beatrice. I think she lives somewhere up north but I'm not sure."

"Is she married?"

Amy shook her head. "No. She did have a fiancé but he died a few years ago in a riding accident. It was very sad."

"Oh, that's awful." Angelina said, genuinely saddened for her misfortune.

"He does have a lady friend who visits quite often though there have been no whispers of an engagement."

"Oh? What's she like?"

Amy pulled a face. "I know it isn't my place to say so, but I really don't like her." She took another bite of the sandwich before continuing, "She's quite pretty. in a haughty sort of way but she walks around as though she has a terrible smell under her nose."

Angelina couldn't help but laugh at Amy's description. "I hope I don't ever have to meet her!"

"I think you will. She visits often and not always with an invite." She tapped her fingers on the table, "It's almost as if she thinks she owns the place."

"That sounds like her intention." Angelina surmised. "What's her name so I know who to look out for?"

"Lady Edwina Honeycutt."

It was Angelina's turn to pull a face. "What an unusual surname!"

Amy giggled, "For an unusual person!"

They both fell about laughing and Angelina's mood improved considerably. This was exactly what she needed.

All she had to do now was get through an afternoon with the formidable Lord Sinclair!

After her lovely light-hearted break from the boring lessons, Angelina made her way down the wide staircase towards the study, where she knew Lord Sinclair would be waiting for her.

She paused outside the carved oak door, taking a deep breath to still her nerves. As defiant as she was, she certainly didn't want to receive another spanking. All she had to do was behave. She could do this!

Raising her hand, she gave a brief knock.

"Come!"

The clipped tone of his voice set her heart racing. Had he forgiven her for yesterday or was he still mad at her? Opening the door, she stepped inside.

Before the warm glow of the fireplace, Lord Sinclair reclined in a tufted leather armchair, engrossed in papers strewn across his polished desk. He looked up, his eyes dark and unfathomable.

Angelina raised her chin slightly to give an air of confidence and approached the desk.

"I trust you had an informative morning with Miss Preston?" The deep timbre of his voice resonated around the room.

"Yes, it was err... very interesting." She said, thinking the complete opposite.

His mouth twitched slightly and Angelina thought for a moment that he found her comment amusing but it disappeared as quickly as it had come. Maybe she had imagined it?

"Well then, take a seat and we shall begin with a reading from Plato." Angelina hid the sigh of dismay that was threatening to erupt. Lord, how tiresome! She felt like throwing herself into the nearest lake. It would be far more exciting!

Instead, she quietly sat down, selected the assigned text and began to read, stumbling slightly over unfamiliar words.

Lord Sinclair listened quietly, correcting Lady Angelina's pronunciations when needed. After half an hour, he noticed she was starting to fidget.

He ignored it at first and found himself instead watching her slender fingers turn the pages. He knew that teaching the willful little madam would be challenging and it had proven to be the case. But that didn't mean that it wasn't enjoyable.

Having her pert little bottom draped over his lap yesterday had left him thinking of little else. He knew he should keep a proper distance, for both their sakes. His position demanded neutrality as her guardian and tutor. But with Angelina, neutrality grew difficult to maintain.

That spark of defiance in her eyes, challenging him even as she obeyed - it stirred a passion in him that he didn't know existed. The rosy blush of her cheeks when vexed was a distraction he found himself revisiting at inopportune moments.

In all truth, her keen wit and fiery nature was something that had been missing in his life. He didn't know that until now. Angelina was a breath of fresh air, reawakening his mind and senses both.

But this fascination could lead nowhere. He was thirteen years older than her, and she deserved a match more fitting for her age.

His mind turned to Lady Edwina. She had made it plain that she wanted to marry him but something had always held him back. Now, sitting across from the delicately beautiful Angelina, he knew why. The two women were like chalk and cheese.

Although Angelina was feisty and determined, there was room for improvement. Edwina was spoiled and selfish, nothing in the world could change that. He also knew her to be false. The way she simpered to him sometimes made him uneasy.

But despite how he felt for Angelina, he would resolve to bury his feelings and remain the mentor that she required.

He watched her fidget again and decided that perhaps for today, she had had enough. He admired her fortitude for he knew deep down that she had no desire to even be there.

"I think that's enough for this afternoon." he said, "I must say I am very impressed with your behaviour today. Miss Preston remarked on how attentive you were at this morning's lessons."

He watched the spark appear in her eyes again but she remained polite, that in itself was an improvement.

He stood up and walked to the door, noting how quickly she followed. No doubt in a hurry to escape his tutorship. Opening the study door, he stepped aside so she could exit the room. "And Lady Angelina, no running in the hallway."

Lord Sinclair closed the door of the study with a smile, wondering if she would obey him or not. He had a feeling the latter would be more apt.

Sure enough, the first clacks of Angelina's heeled slippers were slow and careful. But as the sounds receded down the corridor, they gradually quickened in pace. He listened intently, able to pinpoint her location by the shifting rhythm.

When at last only silence greeted him, Lord Sinclair knew she must have turned the corner in a burst of speed, thinking he could no longer hear her.

For now, he decided to turn a blind eye to her small rebellion but it had been noted and Lord Sinclair never forgot a thing!

It was only mid-afternoon and now Angelina had finished her lesson with Lord Sinclair she would have dearly liked to walk around the gardens. But he had forbidden it.

She stepped out onto the small balcony and placing her hands on the ledge, looked out across the manicured lawns to the soft green hills in the distance. Here, at least, she could get some fresh air. The scenery was breathtaking.

Peering over the ledge she looked down to the ground. Directly below her was a gravel path lined with small shrubs and pretty flowers. The balcony itself wasn't very high. Not high at all. A sly expression crossed her face. If she was just to put one leg over the side, she could easily grip onto the large vine and then climb down.

Looking left and right, she saw no one. So quick as lightning, and before she could change her mind, she swiftly climbed over the ledge, down the vine and within moments landed on the ground as nimbly as a cat. Her heart in her mouth, she took off across the lawn and was soon hidden in the rose garden.

Breathing heavily from not only the exercise but the sense of devilment, she laughed to herself. Good lord, she hoped no one had seen her but this was far too tempting to resist. Fie on Lord Sinclair and his rules!

Soon she was walking amongst the roses, inhaling their heady scent and gorgeous colours. It was truly relaxing. It was all so beautiful and peaceful. Lord Sinclair's groundsmen did a pristine job of tending the large area.

She came across a small bench and laid down, facing the sky. A few wispy clouds dotted the blue canopy and she watched them lazily drift by. It wasn't long before her eyes began to close and she drifted peacefully off into a light slumber.

* * *

"What do you mean your mistress isn't in her room?" Miss Preston snapped.

Amy looked at her with big eyes. "I-I can't find her, Miss."

"Then where is she?"

"I don't rightly know." Amy was as perplexed as she was.

"Dinner is in half an hour and Lady Honeycutt will be joining Lord Sinclair. He will go apoplectic if she turns up late. Or indeed, if she even turns up at all! Willful girl!"

"What should we do?" Amy asked nervously.

"Go and look for her but use caution. I don't wish for Lady Honeycutt to know that Lord Sinclair's ward is so disobedient. It won't reflect well on his authority." Her lips pursed angrily. "Start in the gardens and I will search the other bedrooms in case she has sought sanctuary in one of them."

Amy watched her walk away, muttering under her breath. Lady Angelina was going to be in yet more trouble if she didn't have a good excuse!

* * *

Angelina was having a lovely dream. She was back home, lying on her bed and thinking about where to ride out in the afternoon on her beautiful horse, Ruby. But for some reason the mattress on her bed wasn't as comfortable as usual, in fact, it was quite hard. Her brow furrowed in her sleep and she rolled over onto her side.

She awoke with a start, her cheek pressed uncomfortably against the rough gravel path. Blinking in confusion, the afternoon's events came rushing back and she remembered sitting on the garden bench. Oh, lord she must have fallen asleep!

As she rose, wincing and brushing stray pebbles from her skirt, her maid, Amy came hurrying around the corner. The smile Angelina was going to give was quickly subdued when she saw the panic on Amy's face.

"M'lady, we've been searching everywhere for you!" Amy cried, "dinner will be served soon and Lady Edwina will be in attendance. You must hurry!"

Angelina flushed, imagining the scolding she would receive, if she was found disobeying Lord Sinclair's rules and then a troubling thought occurred to her. "You just said '*we*' have been looking for me? Who is *we*? Please don't say Lord Sinclair!" She grabbed Amy's hands, her eyes wide.

Amy shook her head. "Just me and Miss Preston."

"Miss Preston. Oh, lord, that's just as bad." Her mind schemed quickly. "Look, I'm going back in by the balcony. Give me five minutes and then come into my chambers. Tell her I was there all along. I had pulled the cover up over me on the chaise longue and you didn't see me!"

Amy shrugged. "I can try but she might think I'm a bit daft."

"Please?" Angelina said desperately.

"Very well. But please be careful climbing up that vine!"

They both ran out of the rose garden and making sure the coast was clear, ran across the neat lawns. Angelina heading towards the vine and Amy heading inside the building.

What both of them failed to notice was the elegant lady standing by the corner of the house.

Lady Edwina had thought to take a quick look around the grounds whilst waiting to join Lord Sinclair for dinner. She wanted to take a look at her future holdings, for she intended to own all of it. Lord

Sinclair was proving difficult to ensure but she was a very determined woman and had no intention of giving up.

She had just rounded the corner of the main house when she spied two women running across the lawn. Curiosity made her duck behind the building and peer out to see what they were up to.

One of the women was dressed smartly with her blonde hair pulled back into a knot, the other was clearly a servant, judging by her attire. But why were they running so?

She continued her perusal and when she saw the blonde girl begin to climb the vine up towards a balcony, her mouth gaped open!

Ladies didn't do things like that! Who on earth was that girl? She knew Lord Sinclair had a sister - maybe it was her?

Narrowing her eyes, she decided to ask Lord Sinclair over dinner. Whoever that girl was, he needed to be made aware of her behaviour. It was rather indecent to be behaving in such a fashion, why she had even seen a glimpse of her ankles! Oh, indeed, Lord Sinclair would be mortified to know such a thing was happening under his very nose.

Chapter 4

Lady Angelina was seated at her dressing table having her hair neatly pinned up by Amy, when Miss Preston breezed in.

"Where on earth have you been?" She asked Angelina, her beady eyes taking in her appearance. "You are in so much trouble! When Lord Sinclair hears about this...!"

Angelina quickly interrupted her. "Why am I in trouble? I haven't done anything!"

"We couldn't find you...!"

Again, Angelina interrupted her, "So? That's not my problem. I was here all the time."

"Don't lie to me."

"I'm not!" Angelina shrugged. "I fell asleep on the chaise longue and pulled the cover up over me, so in effect I was invisible."

The battle of wills was clear to see and Angelina knew that Miss Preston couldn't prove for or against what she was saying.

Miss Preston gave a disapproving snort and then admonished Amy. "So you failed to see your mistress asleep on the settee. I should make you go to bed hungry tonight for such an oversight!"

Angelina rounded on her, "That's unfair!"

"Watch your manners, young lady! I will decide what is fair and what isn't." They stared at each other until Angelina turned back to face the mirror so Amy could put the finishing touches to her hair.

Angelina watched Miss Preston in the mirror's reflection, seeing if she would press the issue or not. Thankfully, she chose the latter.

"Dinner is imminent, now make haste. Lord Sinclair will be most displeased if you are late!"

She left the room and both girls collapsed against each other. "Oh my!" Amy breathed. "I didn't think you'd be able to carry that off!"

Angelina giggled. "Thank God I managed to get back into the room without being seen. She cannot prove anything untoward happened now."

Putting the final pin in Angelina's hair, Amy stood back and said, "You look beautiful."

"Thank you, Amy. All I have to do now is get through an evening with Lady Edwina! Wish me luck."

Angelina entered the dining hall with trepidation, dreading meeting the rather imperious sounding Lady Edwina. Lord Sinclair was intimidating enough on his own let alone adding a harpy that wanted him for her husband. She would no doubt see her as a rival.

The woman in question was standing next to Lord Sinclair at the fireplace and she quickly turned when she heard Angelina enter the room. Their eyes met and in that instant, Angelina knew she was going to be trouble. Although quite attractive, her lips were thin hinting at an inner meanness of spirit.

Lady Edwina's eyes swept down Angelina's trim figure, openly appraising her and trying to ascertain if she was a threat to her or not.

Lord Sinclair stepped forward, "Ah there you are, Lady Angelina. I would like to introduce you to Lady Edwina Honeycutt, a neighbour of mine."

"Oh, surely more than a neighbour, Lord Sinclair!" She tapped him with her fan and Angelina immediately noted a look of annoyance cross his face. It was only fleeting but she had most definitely seen it.

Lord Sinclair chose to ignore her remark and continued, "Lady Edwina, this is my ward, Lady Angelina Beaumont."

Angelina nodded her head politely and Lady Edwina returned the gesture, although she could clearly see there was a reluctance to do so. She pitied Lord Sinclair if he did choose her for a wife.

He interrupted her thoughts, "Dinner will be served in a moment, so shall we be seated?" He held his hand out in the direction of the long table and within moments, the servants were pulling out the chairs for them.

The first course arrived, vegetable soup, served with warm bread rolls and Angelina immediately tucked in. It was delicious, as usual.

"I do hope you found your studies productive today, Lady Angelina," Lord Sinclair said.

Edwina cut in before she could reply, "If you include climbing, then yes I am certain they were productive!"

Angelina nearly choked on her soup.

Lord Sinclair frowned, "I am uncertain of your meaning, Lady Edwina."

"I fear your instruction may be failing, Lord Sinclair. I saw her this very afternoon, climbing the vine to her balcony like a commoner."

Angelina swallowed hard and tried to stop her face from flaming but it was too late. Lord Sinclair fixed her with a look and demanded, "Is this true?"

Angelina flushed hotly. "I assure you I have no idea what Lady Edwina is suggesting."

"Oh, yes you do. You can't have forgotten already! I mean to say, what a thing to do - clambering about alone, where any man could see!" Edwina smirked. "Scandalous behavior for someone of your station."

Although Angelina was mortified at Lady Edwina's revelations, she was also angry that she was so obviously enjoying her predicament. Wicked, brazen harpy.

Her heart hammering in her chest, she tried to deny the accusations. "I think you are confusing me with someone else, Lady Edwina."

Lady Edwina turned and looked at her, her eyes sparkling wickedly, "All we have to do is ask the maid that was with you."

"There was no one with me!" Realising what she had just revealed, her eyes widened and she tried to retract her statement, "I mean...!"

"Go to your room!" Lord Sinclair said, his eyes like coal.

"I...!"

"Now!" He thundered.

Her eyes wide, she threw down her napkin and with as much dignity as she could muster, exited the dining hall. Oh lord, she had thought herself safe from her antics earlier but it wasn't the case. Far from it!

Running quickly up the winding staircase, she entered her chambers and threw herself face down on the bed. Not only was she being denied her dinner but she knew, without a doubt, that she would soon receive discipline from Lord Sinclair.

The thought made her stomach flip with a mixture of excitement and trepidation. She rolled onto her back and looked up at the textured ceiling, puzzled by her feelings. What had made her think that it was exciting? She pulled in her bottom lip with her small teeth. Why did the prospect of going over his lap again, cause such an emotion in her. The command in his voice, the having to submit to his authority. Dear Lord, was she going mad?

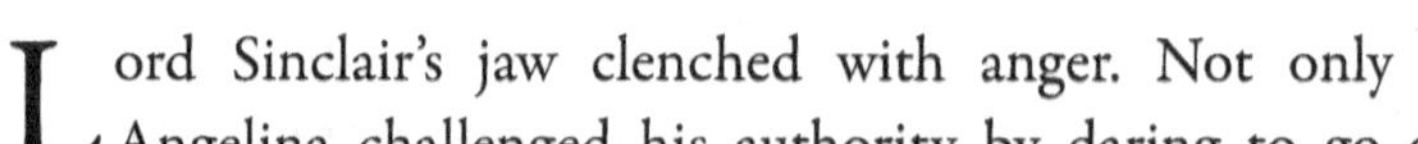

Lord Sinclair's jaw clenched with anger. Not only had Lady Angelina challenged his authority by daring to go out in the gardens which he had expressly forbidden but she had put her very life in danger by climbing up to the balcony. He had never known anyone so stubborn or willful.

Just when he thought she was beginning to change her ways, this happened.

He rubbed his forehead, trying to suppress his anger so he could get through the rest of the evening with Lady Edwina. In all truth his hand was itching to smack Lady Angelina's bottom into submission.

Hopefully, the defiant little madam was now worrying about what punishment he would mete out.

"You appear troubled, Lord Sinclair. I hope I am not the cause, for I do think I had a duty to inform you of her behaviour. It isn't seemly for a lady to be seen doing such things."

Lord Sinclair suppressed a sigh. It was clear that Lady Edwina was taking pleasure from his ward's behaviour. There was only a few years between them and she would take Angelina as a rival.

Although, maybe in that assumption she was correct.

"Now we can speak freely, my lord," Lady Edwina trilled, laying a hand on his arm. "Without that chit distracting you."

Lord Sinclair extracted himself politely. "Lady Angelina is a bright young woman, and under my protection. I would ask you to treat her with respect, if you please."

Lady Edwina waved away his rebuke. "She will learn her place, as all women must. But come, let us speak of more pleasant things. When shall we announce our engagement?"

Good grief. She was even more brazen tonight than usual. He tried to be as polite as possible but also firm. "I believe I have made my position clear, Lady Edwina. I am not presently seeking a wife."

Her eyes narrowed a little, "You must take a wife at some point, my lord and I am a most advantageous match." She fluttered her eyelashes at him and tried to act coy but he knew her too well by now. It was all a ruse.

The last course arrived and thankfully, Lady Edwina ceased talking for a moment to delight over the exquisite dessert.

Lady Edwina was a headache he didn't need, and her scorn for Angelina made him realise what an awful woman she truly was.

Half an hour later and finally he was alone, Lady Edwina having departed in her carriage.

Walking into the haven of his study, Lord Sinclair sat down and poured himself a brandy. Swirling the amber liquid around in the glass, he mulled over his ward's behaviour and what he was going to do about it.

There was a sharp knock at Angelina's chamber door and her heart leapt nervously. She knew without a doubt who it was.

Licking her suddenly very dry lips, she called out, "Enter."

Lord Sinclair stepped inside, his presence immediately foreboding. Angelina clasped her hands together anxiously wondering if perhaps she was worrying unnecessarily but one look at his face, told her all she needed to know. His expression was stern and unyielding and she knew she was in a whole world of trouble. Her buttocks clenched in anticipation.

Perhaps she could appeal to his better side but as soon as he spoke, she knew it wasn't going to work. She didn't even know why she had thought it would.

"So," he began, "even though I told you not to go into the gardens, you still thought it quite acceptable to disobey me?"

She lowered her gaze, chastened. "I know it looks like that, my lord but in all truth, I wasn't out there long. I didn't wander far, just enough to take in the surroundings. It just happened that Lady Edwina saw me." Unfortunately for me, she thought. Talk about bad timing!

"And what about climbing up the vine to the balcony? I presume you made your way down the same way." His eyes bore into hers, his disapproval apparent.

"Well, I suppose that was rather foolish and reckless." she sneaked a look at him, wondering if her speech would make him more lenient.

But it wasn't to be. His jaw was firmly set, his brows low. Oh, lord.

"Do you actually think you can do as you like?" he asked curiously.

"Of course not, but if no one had seen me then there would be no problem, would there!" she snapped irritably.

"Watch your tone, my Lady!" he admonished her sharply. "You are in enough trouble already without giving me attitude!"

She looked down at the carpet and thrust out her bottom lip.

He continued, his tone harsh. "Must I remind you, yet again, that you have been sent here to amend your ways? Do you think climbing up and down vines is an improvement? Well? Answer me!"

Angelina shuffled her feet and refused to meet his gaze. This wasn't going great. Not great at all. She managed to mutter a subdued, "No."

For a moment there was silence and then she looked up when she heard him open the door. "You will follow me down to the study and woe betide you if you dare to disobey!"

She watched as he strode out of the room and with a loud huff, did as he had ordered. She knew her punishment was imminent and didn't wish to make it any worse.

⁂

Lord Sinclair opened his study door and ushered the wayward Lady Angelina inside. Her little form was stiff and her eyes were yet rebellious. But he would soon make her think twice before disobeying him again.

He pulled out a chair and placed it in the middle of the room just in front of her.

He saw her eyes widen and she took a step backwards. Before she could utter a word, his hand snaked out, and grabbing her wrist, he swiftly pulled her down over his lap as he seated himself.

She let out a little yelp of surprise and tried to wriggle off.

"Truly, you don't have to do this! I have learned my lesson." She said, her voice straining a little.

"No, you haven't but you will, I assure you." He warned.

He quickly raised her skirts and threw them over her back, revealing her lacy white bloomers. Parting the material, he exposed her silky curves. He couldn't help but admire the plump cheeks that he was about to punish. They were perfect.

He raised his hand and brought it smacking down on both cheeks. He heard her suck in a breath and it gave him a certain satisfaction that she would now pay for her disobedience.

He smacked her again and then again, setting up a steady rhythm that soon had her writhing on his lap, trying to escape.

"Oh, please, my lord, it hurts! I won't do it again!"

He ignored her and continued the onslaught, catching the tops of her thighs and then her sit spots. When he saw her bottom change to a blushing shade of pink, he paused, letting his hand remain on her sizzling smooth skin.

"Now, you are going to position yourself over my desk and take several strokes of the cane." He pulled her up to stand in front of him. "And the more you argue, the more you will receive!"

Angelina stared at him, her eyes wide, her lower lip pulled in. He meant every word.

She thought about protesting but knew it would fall on deaf ears. She had never had the cane. The mere thought was terrifying!

He walked her to his desk, where she lowered herself reluctantly over the cold surface. As her cheek lay against the cool wood, she winced. Why on earth couldn't she just learn to do as she was told?

Because at home, she got away with it. That was why. But she was finding out that Lord Sinclair was not so easy to manipulate. Oh no indeed.

Her skirts lifted onto her back, she felt his hands pull her bloomers down to pool at her ankles. She shuffled her feet nervously. Oh, lord!

She watched him walk to a tall polished cabinet where he pulled out a long, thin, crook-handled cane. He flicked it through the air and her stomach flipped at the loud swishing sound. Oh, God. This wasn't going to be good.

His eyes locked with hers and she shivered, unable to tear her gaze away as he approached her side. He moved out of her vision and she felt his hand lay on the small of her back. She grit her teeth and nervously awaited the first cut.

Thwack!

She gasped as the stinging line of pain filled her senses. Oh my, it was worse than she had envisioned.

Thwack!

"Ohhhhh!" she hissed, gripping the desk tightly. The sensation was intense and it took all her willpower to remain in position.

Another two followed in quick succession and she quickly tried to rise up but Lord Sinclair kept her firmly held down with just one hand. She slipped her own hand around and rubbed one of her buttocks, kicking her legs up as she tried to handle the fiery sting.

"Take your hand away! Now!" he ordered.

Angelina reluctantly did as she was bid and closed her eyes tightly, awaiting the next stroke.

Thwack!

At the last stroke, Lord Sinclair allowed her to jump up. Her face was screwed up with pain and she practically danced on the spot as she tried to alleviate the soreness in her bottom.

"Oh, my, that really hurts!" she wailed. "You had no right to do that!"

"I suggest you apologise… unless, of course, you want some more?" He swished the cane in the air threateningly.

She quickly shook her head and responded, "I'm sorry."

Lord Sinclair looked at her, trying to assess whether she was truly repentant or just trying to avoid further punishment.

Maybe it was a bit of both. She was certainly proving to be a challenge. Her precocious nature was hard to tame.

He looked at her full lips, pouting with self pity and imagined what it would be like to kiss them. Annoyed with himself he pushed it from his thoughts. He was here to educate and instruct her, and being a man of good standing and reliability that is just what he intended to do.

Putting the cane back in the cabinet, he walked over to her. "If you dare to even think about doing something so foolhardy again, I will have no hesitation in dragging you straight back here and leaning you over that desk. Do you understand?"

She nodded and looked at him with wide eyes. He thought he detected a hint of desire within their shining blue depths but surely not? Maybe that was just wishful thinking on his behalf.

He walked to the door and opened it, "Now, you are to go straight to bed and I expect you to attend lessons as usual in the morning. If you are late, I will know."

She went to walk past him and stopped, looking up at him with big eyes, "May I ask that you don't reprimand, Amy, my maid. She was only following me and had no say in what I did."

He nodded. "Very well."

When she had left, he thought about that look in her eyes. Did she feel the connection they had as well?

He walked over and poured himself a brandy. A stiff drink was just what he needed to quell his irrational thoughts. It was late and he was tired, that must be it. He was imagining things that weren't there.

Tossing the drink down his throat, he left his study and retired to his rooms.

Chapter 5

Angelina had been at Withdean for over a week but it felt more like two. She was doing her best to adhere to all the rules but was finding it so difficult.

Amy was proving to be more of a friend than a maid, and her funny anecdotes made the days go by much more quickly. Since her last punishment she had made sure to behave properly, as best she could. That blasted cane had hurt so much, she had no desire to experience that again!

Mornings were filled with the prim Miss Preston and an hour or two in the afternoon she was tutored by Lord Sinclair. She sometimes had problems concentrating on his words because she found herself admiring his handsome features. She knew she shouldn't but couldn't help herself. And he had many an occasion to chastise her for her lack of concentration.

She giggled to herself. If only he knew her true thoughts!

Lord Sinclair had finally lifted the ban on going into the garden, and so now she could freely walk along the lawns and gardens in her free time. It was so beautiful and peaceful.

She looked up as Amy entered her chambers. "M'lady, you are going to be late for this morning's lessons unless you get a move on." She tutted and walked over to her. Taking her hand she pulled her off the bed and thrust her towards the door. "Move!" She laughed good naturedly.

Angelina groaned but knew that Amy was right. Once out of the door, she made her way downstairs and her next boring lesson with Miss Preston. Hopefully, not many more of these and she could return to her own home, a reformed character. Or so her father would believe.

The morning started off fairly well, although it was one of Angelina's least favourite things to do - embroidery. Her work was passable but it was nothing like her sister's which was perfect. Or indeed Miss Preston's.

But her frustration with Miss Preston had almost reached a boiling point. All she did was criticise. Honestly! Couldn't she find one thing nice to say? She glanced at her governess from beneath her lashes, wondering why she was so mean and in the process pricked her finger yet again.

"Ouch!" She hissed and sucked on the tiny bubble of blood that appeared.

"If you concentrated more, that wouldn't happen!" Miss Preston reprimanded her. "You are forever daydreaming."

"Must you find fault in everything I do?" Angelina snapped, glaring at her.

Miss Preston's eyes narrowed to flint. "Mind your attitude, my lady. Else I decide that you require stricter discipline."

Angelina swiftly went silent. If word got back to Lord Sinclair about her behaviour, then she knew what sort of discipline would be administered. She shifted uncomfortably on her chair imagining his large hands making contact with her backside.

She spent the rest of the morning doing her best and in the end, she managed to produce something quite passable. Even if she did say so herself.

When the morning ended, she quickly headed to her chambers for a well deserved respite.

After a satisfying light lunch, Amy entered her chambers to clear away the plates. Angelina thanked her and quickly noticed a gleam in her eye.

"What are you smiling about, Amy? Do tell!"

Amy quickly took a seat at the table and leaning near, she whispered, "M'lady, have you heard? The village is holding a grand barn dance tonight to celebrate the summer solstice!"

Angelina perked up at the news, "A dance? Oh, how lovely! I haven't been to a dance in quite a while." Her face fell, "I would love to attend but I don't suppose it will be allowed."

Amy lowered her voice. "Who's to stop you? If you sneak away after dark, no one will find out. Lord Sinclair retires well before midnight. I could meet you at the garden gate at midnight."

The idea was tantalizing, yet Angelina hesitated, "If I were caught, the consequences..."

"Please, m'lady? I would love you to experience it. It's such fun!" Amy gave her best pleading look. "I'll help fashion a disguise and keep watch, I promise no harm will come."

Angelina wavered, longing for adventure beyond the manor's walls. She had been the perfect ward for over a week now and to be honest it was getting boring. A dance was just what she needed to liven up her dreary existence having to listen to Miss Preston every day! Perhaps a small rebellion would do no real harm.

Her mind made up, she said excitedly, "Very well, I will come. But you must swear to me, Amy - our secret will be kept safe!"

Amy beamed. "On my honour, m'lady. Now let's plan your costume!"

━━━━━━━━ ❧ ━━━━━━━━

Midnight had come, and Lady Angelina slipped out of her room silently and stole through the dark corridors with baited breath.

Amy had told her the small side door would be open and it was the best way to leave the house undetected.

Even though she was breaking the rules, the thrill of the oncoming night was beyond exciting!

Slipping out of the side door, she ran lightly across the lawns to meet Amy by the garden gate as planned.

"You came!" Amy whispered, embracing her. "I thought for one minute you might change your mind."

Angelina threw back her hood to reveal herself, disguised in Amy's plain dress, a long cape and with her hair hanging loose about her face, she was transformed. "How do I look? Will I pass for a simple village maid?" Her eyes sparkled wickedly in the moonlight.

"You look simply perfect!" Amy giggled. "Come, the music and dancing awaits!"

They hurried through moonlit fields, arriving breathless at the big barn situated just outside the village where loud music could be heard and people's laughter filling the air. Angelina's heart soared. This was exactly what she needed. Walking inside, she watched couples spin and stomp to lively fiddles.

This party stood in stark contrast to the formal balls she typically attended. Amy eagerly ushered her through the entrance, and before long, a glass of an unfamiliar tipple was placed into her hand. Although she couldn't discern its exact nature, its flavour was delightful!

As the night progressed, Angelina sampled the local wines and ales with Amy's friends. It was rather fun not to be so straight laced and conform to silly rules all the time. There was no deference or curtseying, no hesitation in how they spoke to her. It was truly refreshing.

"Amy, this is so much fun!" She giggled, sampling some more of the heady wine. She felt a little dizzy but the feeling was quite welcome. Any inhibitions she had just simply disappeared.

All too soon, Amy was steering her homewards as the moon began to set. Dawn was merely an hour away. As their laughter rang through the forest paths, another sound reached them - the snap of branches. They spun around to find Lord Sinclair astride his stallion, eyes glinting sternly in the moonlight.

"Explain yourselves at once," he commanded. The girls froze in their tracks, like deer caught in lamplight. Angelina suddenly felt sick to the stomach! Oh, Lord. How the devil had he found out they had left the house? But there was no time for wondering that now, the fact was he was here and he was angry.

"My lord, we can explain -" Amy began, but Lord Sinclair silenced her with a glare.

"You will explain nothing. Return home at once before worse befalls you!" Amy squeezed Angelina's hand and then fled without a backward glance. One didn't argue with Lord Sinclair!

Angelina swayed on the spot, the heady wine still circulating throughout her body and not thinking straight, she decided to make a dash for home.

She heard Lord Sinclair mutter an expletive before he quickly dismounted and caught her in his muscular arms. Without a word, he hoisted her before him with ease onto the large stallion, ignoring her slurred protests.

"Be silent," he growled, spurring the horse into motion. Holding onto her with one arm wrapped around her slender body, she had no choice but to cling onto him as he cantered towards home.

Lord Sinclair held the petite woman in his arms as he cantered along the track. She looked so different with her hair tumbling down her back, free of its usual restraints. Her delicate perfume wafted up to him and despite his disappointment in her behaviour, he couldn't help but recognise his attraction towards her.

He was just thankful he had found out about her disappearance from the house. It was Maude who had initially discovered her absence. In the early hours before dawn, she had ventured to stoke the fire in Lady Angelina's chambers only to discover her bed had not been slept in. Swiftly, Maude relayed this disconcerting news to Wilson, who in turn made certain he was informed.

At first, he thought she may have run away as she had often threatened. But then, by chance, he happened upon them on the path towards home.

Her disobedient behaviour would be dealt with in the morning but for now, he was thankful to have her in his arms.

Feeling her small body against his, stirred his emotions like no other woman ever had. For a moment he imagined kissing her perfect plump little lips, claiming her for his own. The thought made him frown. He had tried to push such thoughts from his mind and had succeeded so far, but now, with her in such close proximity it was hard to deny how he truly felt.

Urging his stallion into a gallop, he decided that the sooner he returned home, the better.

⁓◦⊙◦⁓

Angelina awoke with the sun shining through the window, though the bright rays made her wince. Raising a hand to her head, she wondered why it ached so and then the memories of the night before came flooding back. The dancing had been wonderful, the atmosphere electric, it had been such fun and then her eyes widened. Oh, no! Lord Sinclair!

She quickly sat up in bed and then groaned when her head began to throb even more. What had she done? She remembered riding home, sitting astride his large horse and the feel of his powerful arm wrapped around her to stop her from falling.

She blushed profusely as her thoughts took a different turn. Lord, it had felt quite exciting, dare she admit. His body was hard and muscular, his scent, a heady mix of oak wood and leather. Seated so close she couldn't help but admire how strong he was.

Placing a hand over her mouth, she wondered if she wasn't beginning to fall in love with him. He certainly set her heart fluttering. But could she fall for such a strict man? A man who thought nothing of putting her over his knee?

Collapsing back down onto her pillows, she closed her eyes and groaned. What a mess she had made for herself!

A knock came on the door and Angelina, called out "Enter!" It was unusual for Amy to knock, so she wasn't surprised when Maude entered the room, carrying a jug of hot water and a fresh towel.

"Lord Sinclair told me not to awaken you early, m'lady and to tell you that your lessons will begin at eleven."

Angelina looked at the clock and her eyes widened when she saw the time. It was already past ten o'clock. She was surprised he was being so forgiving. But then her stomach roiled nervously when Maude added, "He says you are to join him in the study when you're ready."

She groaned and closed her eyes, knowing full well what that meant!

She waited until Maude had put down the jug before asking why Amy wasn't attending her as usual.

"She's been dismissed, m'lady."

"Dismissed!" Angelina gasped. "But she can't have!"

"Oh, yes. Lord Sinclair spoke with her early this morning and she left soon afterwards with her bags packed. She's gone back to her family in the village."

Angelina slipped her legs from beneath the covers and even though her head felt like a lead weight, she got out of bed and said, "Help me dress, make haste!"

"Certainly, m'lady."

With a quick wash and grabbing the first dress that came to hand, Angelina was soon ready to face Lord Sinclair. How dare he dismiss the lovely Amy. She would do everything in her power to demand he reinstate her.

Lord Sinclair was sitting behind his desk when he bid her entry. He regarded her sternly, his face unmoving, waiting for her to speak.

For a moment Angelina felt intimidated but her concern for Amy was far too strong to worry about herself. She raised her chin and asked, "Why have you dismissed Amy, my lord?"

"I should think Amy is the least of your worries at this present time." he said sternly.

She narrowed her eyes, starting to get vexed. "Amy has become very dear to me and I think it very cruel of you to just let her go like that!"

"Do you? Then you still have a lot to learn." He rose and gazed out the window before continuing, "A servant must uphold the highest standards of decorum, as an example to their masters. Discretion and diligence are expected in this household above all else."

He turned around and stared at her. "I had given her fair warning and been far too lenient this past couple of weeks with her behaviour. In this society, one small indiscretion can spread like wildfire and I will not have any whisper of scandal touching this family's good name or yours for that matter."

She kept her eyes downcast for fear he would see the rebellion within and tried to appease him. "I understand and you have every right to be angry with her but it is me you should chastise, my lord. I showed poor judgment in disobeying your rules."

"Poor judgment is an understatement." His voice was ice. "Do you comprehend how your reckless behaviour last night could have reflected upon your name? What might have occurred if someone had recognised you?"

Angelina trembled, anger flooding her being, "I cannot excuse my actions, but I can beg you to reconsider Amy's dismissal. It won't happen again, you have my sworn word."

"Now, why doesn't that fill me with confidence?" He folded his arms across his chest and looked even more imposing than usual.

But Angelina was too angry to back down. "If you don't let her come back, then I shall run away!"

"Where would you go?" His steely eyes looked into hers.

Angelina balled her fists by her side, "I don't know but I will."

"I can see your studies are going to have to become even stricter. You don't seem to have learned much at all, do you?"

Angelina gasped. Stricter! No, no, no! "Oh, I've had enough of this! I'm leaving!" she turned and stormed over to the door but Lord Sinclair rushed over and grabbed her arm.

"Oh, no you don't. You don't get to walk away so easily." He drew her over to the desk and taking a seat, he pulled her straight down over his lap. She wriggled and fought but nothing was going to stop him.

"You cannot have everything your own way, Lady Angelina."

"Let me go! Let me go!" She gritted her teeth. She was so angry.

She soon found her skirts flung over her back and his hands on her bloomers; parting the fabric to expose her bottom.

"You cannot do this again! Unhand me this instant!" She cried, trying her best to escape. But he was far too strong and he soon had one muscular arm wrapped around her waist to hold her in place.

"Silence! After your recent behavior, you cannot expect anything else. You don't seem to learn from your mistakes but you will!"

His hand fell down onto her backside and within minutes it felt like a furnace. His hands were huge. The loud slaps echoed around the wood paneled study, mingled with her shrieks of outrage.

"Ow! Please stop! Ouch!"

"You only have yourself to blame! I will stop when I am good and ready."

She could hear the steely determination in his voice. Each word punctuated by yet another smack to her sore bottom.

"I will not be able to take my lessons if you punish me so!" she protested.

"Oh, you will and I will tell Miss Preston to make you sit on a hard wooden chair this afternoon so that you will remember how to behave as befits a lady!"

"You are being unfair, my lord! Ouch!" her voice rose as he spanked her on her sit spot.

Finally he stopped and pulled her up to sit on his lap. She tried to rise up but he pushed her back down. She grimaced as her sore bottom touched his trousers.

"Hurts does it?" he asked, his voice stern and unwavering.

Angelina nodded, feeling miserable. Not only from the pain in her tender bottom but the fact that she wouldn't be seeing Amy any longer. And both problems were caused by the very man before her.

She glanced up at him and was startled to see a look of disappointment in his eyes. For some reason it made her feel sad, as though she had let him down somehow but she immediately admonished herself. How could she feel such a thing for a man that had just made her backside feel like she was sitting on hot coals?

Lord Sinclair stared at his little ward. He was reluctant to release her from her position on his lap as having her so close was something he relished and maybe such close proximity would make her listen to him more.

Her vibrant blue eyes stared up at him and placing his finger under her chin, he said, "There will be no more talk of you running away, ever. Do you hear?"

Her shoulders slumped and she nodded.

"As for Amy, I will see about reinstating her but only when you have returned home. I feel her influence is far too much of a distraction."

He noticed her eyes light up a little.

"Now, you have even more of a reason to change your ways. Speaking of which, your behaviour last night must not happen again. Do you understand?"

"Yes, my lord." She lowered her lashes, effectively hiding her expression. Whether or not she obeyed him, would remain to be seen.

"Well then, Miss Preston is waiting for you in the music room. I believe she wishes to see what language skills you have."

He noticed she went to roll her eyes and then stopped, catching herself mid roll. He silently laughed to himself. At least she was trying.

She arose from his lap and adjusted her skirts before heading to the door.

"Don't forget to sit on the wooden chair, Lady Angelina. I shall make a point of asking Miss Preston later to make sure you did."

Her lips tightened but she refrained from replying and nodded her head politely before exiting the room. Her perfume still lingered and Lord Sinclair closed his eyes for a moment, savouring the light scent. She was getting under his skin and when the time came for her to leave, would he be able to part with her? Only time would tell.

Chapter 6

Lady Edwina was still simmering over her dinner with Lord Sinclair and his blatant disregard for her feelings. How could he turn her down like that? And what a thing to say - that he wasn't seeking a wife. Whatever next. Every man needed a woman in his life. Especially one of her standing.

She paced the parlour with a renewed determination to secure Lord Sinclair's affections and rid herself of Lady Angelina's competition. She knew she had to devise a plan, something that would not only captivate Lord Sinclair but also expose Lady Angelina's true intentions.

That girl might be there under the ruse of being his ward, but that look in her eyes went far deeper than maybe even Lord Sinclair himself knew.

Lady Edwina summoned her maid, Amelia, to her side. "Amelia, I have a task for you. I need you to discreetly gather information about Lady Angelina Beaumont. Find out everything you can about her past, her connections, and any secrets that she may be hiding." She pictured Lady Angelina's pretty face and her eyes narrowed, "I will bet she has some skeletons hidden in her cupboard!"

Amelia nodded, her eyes filled with loyalty and dedication. "Very well, my lady. I shall do my best. Someone in the village may have some information that may be of use to you."

Lady Edwina smiled, grateful for Amelia's unwavering support. "Thank you, Amelia. Your assistance is invaluable to me. Together, we shall expose Lady Angelina's true nature and ensure Lord Sinclair sees her for who she really is."

And then he shall be mine, she thought to herself, her eyes turning dark with malevolence.

A few days later, Amelia approached her in the gardens. "Lady Edwina, I have some information for you regarding Lady Angelina."

"Oh, you do? Well, come over to the rose garden and we can speak without being overheard."

Once settled, Amelia began to tell her what she had heard in the haberdashery in town. "My lady, I happened to bump into Lord Sinclair's maid, Maude and she said she had overheard whispers amongst the staff that Lady Angelina was sent to Lord Sinclair's care for correction and discipline. It is said that she was caught canoodling with a stable lad at a rather scandalous party!"

Lady Edwina's heart skipped a beat as the pieces of the puzzle started to fit together. "So, she is a strumpet! A devious harlot with a ruined reputation!"

So, her reservations were justified. Lady Angelina's seemingly innocent facade began to crumble, revealing a darker side to her character.

The only problem was that surely Lord Sinclair knew of her misdemeanors. Or did he? Maybe her parents had sent her there under false pretences. The plot thickened.

Armed with this newfound knowledge, Lady Edwina devised a plan to bring Lady Angelina's true intentions to light. She would host an intimate gathering at her family estate, inviting Lord Sinclair, Lady Angelina, and a select group of influential individuals from London's elite circle.

Oh yes, one way or another she would show Lady Angelina up for the trollope that she was!

----- ❧ -----

Lord Sinclair sat at his desk a few days later and read the invitation from Lady Edwina. Wilson had discreetly placed the delicate envelope on the edge of his desk earlier but upon seeing the wax seal bearing Lady Edwina's family crest, Lord Sinclair had pushed it aside.

After a while though, curiosity had made him open the damned thing. His eyes scanned the elegant calligraphy that adorned the page. It was an invitation to a small soirée, hosted by Lady Edwina at her family estate. He inwardly groaned and continued reading and then one name caught his attention - Lady Angelina.

A flicker of confusion crossed Lord Sinclair's face as he pondered Lady Edwina's intentions. Why would she include Lady Angelina in such an event? He knew she considered her a rival for his affections, even though he had told her he had no intention of taking a wife at the moment.

His mind raced with questions, and a feeling of unease settled in his chest.

He couldn't help but wonder if Lady Edwina had some ulterior motive, a hidden agenda behind extending an invitation to Lady Angelina. Could it be a ploy to humiliate her somehow? After all, she had seemed to take pleasure in exposing Lady Angelina's rather scandalous behaviour last time.

Lord Sinclair rubbed his chin, thinking hard. He didn't quite trust Lady Edwina but now he questioned her true intentions.

As he stared at the invitation, his mind conjured up an array of possibilities - none of them good. Unless of course, Lady Edwina was doing it by way of an apology for getting Lady Angelina into trouble?

He shook his head. That option, he very much doubted.

With a heavy sigh, Lord Sinclair folded the invitation and placed it back on his desk. The weight of the decision ahead sat heavily on his shoulders as he grappled with conflicting emotions. Should he attend the soirée and see what happened? Or should he decline the invitation, fearing the potential harm it could bring?

He poured himself a brandy and swirling the amber liquid around in the glass, he sat pondering his predicament. Lady Angelina had to go back into society at some point and at least, if he was there by her side, he could protect her.

With a determined glint in his eyes, Lord Sinclair resolved to attend the soirée and challenge any problems head on.

Besides, accompanying Lady Angelina to a soirée was certainly not a chore, not at all. It would give him great pleasure.

As the evening of the gathering approached, Angelina grew more nervous. She distrusted Lady Edwina completely and had no desire to be in her company. Not one bit. But the idea of an evening out and dressing up in one of her finer gowns was very appealing.

And she couldn't deny the excitement of being Lord Sinclair's partner for the evening. Lady Edwina might want him for her own but she would be the one by his side. That would hopefully make her jealous which would be a good pay back for her snitching about seeing her climbing the vines.

Maude added the final touches to Angelina's hair and shot her a brief smile. She was no replacement for Amy. Oh, how she missed her little maid. But not long now and she would be able to come back and take up her position. It was up to Angelina to behave and prove herself a redeemed character. She could do this!

She nodded at her reflection in the mirror and then taking a deep breath, stood up and headed to the door. Maude handed her a fan and placed a delicate shawl around her shoulders. "There, m'lady, you are ready."

Her skirts swished as she left the room and began the descent down the stairs. Lord Sinclair was waiting at the bottom and she paused for a moment to admire him. Looking resplendent in a black suit, crisp white shirt and burgundy embroidered waistcoat and cravat, he looked more handsome than ever.

She breathed deeply to calm her erratic pulse as she began her descent of the grand staircase once more. At the bottom, her eyes met those of Lord Sinclair, who had glanced up at that very moment.

Time seemed to pause. In his intense gaze, she saw a warmth and interest that mirrored her own feelings. Did he too feel the connection between them?

Stepping forward with graceful courtesy, he extended his arm. "My Lady Angelina, our carriage awaits. I will escort you."

She placed her hand on his sleeve with a small smile. "I confess I am a little nervous about tonight's soirée. What if Lady Edwina says something nasty or unkind?"

He patted her hand. "I will be by your side so push such thoughts from your mind. Take tonight for what it is, an enjoyable soirée amongst friends."

And so they walked to the waiting carriage and once settled, the wheels started to trundle along the gravel drive but Angelina couldn't quell the feeling of unease. Lady Edwina was more wicked than Lord Sinclair believed. She was certain of it. One thing was for sure, she would keep her wits about her this evening!

Lady Edwina had meticulously planned every detail. The grand ballroom was adorned with exquisite floral arrangements, and she had hired the finest musicians to serenade her guests. No matter the size of her social gatherings, she always made certain to impress.

She glanced down at her gown, it had been made to the highest standards, a breathtaking creation of silk and lace, making her the centre of attention as she greeted her guests with grace and charm.

Among the guests was Lord Sinclair. Her eyes lit up at the sight of him and she only just about managed to hide a scowl when she saw Lady Angelina standing by his side. Walking up to them she bid them welcome.

"I am so glad you could come." She said, fluttering her lashes at Lord Sinclair and totally ignoring Lady Angelina.

A waiter came forward with a tray of champagne and she handed one to both of them. "Do enjoy yourselves. If you will excuse me, I must greet my other guests." She breezed off regally towards the entrance.

After a sumptuous seven course dinner, the men moved to the study for cigars and brandy, the women to the parlour, for tea and coffee.

Without Lord Sinclair by her side, Angelina felt a little bereft but thankfully the two glasses of wine she had during her meal, subdued her nerves somewhat. She opted for a cup of coffee and took a seat on one of the settees next to an elderly lady.

The old lady openly admired her dress, "You look very beautiful, my dear."

Angelina smiled, "Thank you."

"I haven't seen you before. From where do you hail?"

"Langley Vale. My family live at Highfold Manor."

"Oh, how lovely. I have visited that town many times. I am Lady Millicent Montgomery."

"Lady Angelina, very pleased to meet you." Angelina gave her a genuine smile, immediately feeling a connection between them.

Lady Edwina sauntered over and upon hearing the end of their conversation added, "Yes, Lady Angelina is Lord Sinclair's ward."

"Oh? If you don't mind me saying, Lady Angelina, you seem a little old to be a ward. What are you? Twenty? Twenty-one?" Lady Millicent said, looking slightly puzzled.

Angelina swallowed hard. "I am twenty-one. My father sent me to Lord Sinclair for extra instruction. He is such an esteemed member of society and my father felt that his guidance would be beneficial to me."

Good lord, she hoped that would quell any gossip.

Lady Millicent nodded her head. "Your father sounds like a very wise man. I have known Lord Sinclair for many years and he is one of the finest men I know."

"Oh, indeed, he is so knowledgeable and trustworthy," Lady Edwina said and then casting a sly look at Angelina, added, "But maybe he is a little too trusting for his own good."

Angelina glanced at her, immediately sensing danger. She noted the evil glint in Lady Edwina's eyes and knew that she was out to cause trouble. Just as she had thought!

Lady Millicent seemed a little annoyed at Lady Edwina's comment and immediately rebuked her, "Lord Sinclair knows whom to trust I am sure. He is not a man to be trifled with and I certainly wouldn't think anyone could dupe someone of his calibre!"

Angelina couldn't help a look of satisfaction cross her face as she pointedly looked at Lady Edwina.

Lady Edwina's eyes narrowed with spite and raising her voice slightly so others could hear, she remarked, "I am not so sure, Lady Millicent. I couldn't help but overhear a rather scandalous rumour the other day."

The other ladies present, eager for a juicy story, leaned in closer, their eyes gleaming with anticipation.

"My dear friends," Lady Edwina began, thoroughly enjoying having an audience and being the centre of attention, "It seems that there is a certain lady in our vicinity who has been caught in a compromising position."

Gasps of astonishment rippled through the group, and Lady Edwina revelled in the attention she had garnered. She couldn't help but steal a glance in Angelina's direction.

Angelina stared at her with a mixture of consternation and horror. What on earth did she think she would gain by exposing her so?

Lady Millicent noted the look between them and knew what was going on immediately.

"It is said," Lady Edwina continued, her tone dripping with faux concern, "that this lady was discovered canoodling with none other than a lowly stable boy. Can you imagine the scandal?"

As the whispers and murmurs spread throughout the parlour, Lady Edwina pointedly looked at Lady Angelina and was about to say something else when Lady Millicent interrupted.

"That is quite enough gossip for one evening, Lady Edwina. I haven't come here to talk about stable boys and the like. Your soirées are known for their dancing and fine music are they not? So come, let us transfer to your beautiful ballroom."

The other ladies attention was immediately diverted to the delightful prospect of dancing and the idle gossip was quickly forgotten - for now. They began exiting the parlour, talking excitedly. Lady Edwina was swept up with them, as they wanted her to urge the men to hurry and join them. For one needed a partner to have a dance!

Angelina remained where she was, relieved that her name had not been revealed. But it would have been, if not for Lady Millicent. She glanced at the old lady, still seated and sipping her tea daintily. She was staring at Angelina with an understanding look and nodded imperceptibly. Angelina shot her a small thankful smile back.

Her stomach roiled nervously, her feelings a mixture of mortification and dismay. She knew that Lady Edwina would tell her friends at some point and wondered how she would endure their ridicule. She blinked back the tears that threatened to fall.

How the devil had she found out about her indiscretion?

Her bottom lip trembled and she pressed her lips tightly together. She wouldn't give in to the tears, it would mean that Lady Edwina had won.

Walking over to the window, she looked out in a trance, her mind in too much turmoil to admire the view. All she wanted to do now was go home. Her evening was ruined.

Lord Sinclair finished his cigar, savoring the rich aroma that filled the air. He took one last sip of brandy, allowing its warmth to spread through his veins. Some of the men had left the study already, to the delight of the young women waiting for them in the ballroom. The night was still young, and there was plenty of dancing to be had.

He, himself, was looking forward to a dance with Lady Angelina. She looked exquisite this evening and it would be his greatest pleasure to lead her around the ballroom in a dance of her choosing.

His face softened, thinking of her. She had held herself with such grace throughout dinner, she could not be faulted. She had truly made an effort with her lessons this past week and he knew it wouldn't be long before she would be leaving.

The thought filled him with sadness.

Excusing himself from the company of his fellow gentlemen left in the room, he made his way through the grand hallways of Lady Edwina's estate, his footsteps echoing against the polished marble floors.

As he approached the ballroom, the sound of laughter and music grew louder. However, to his surprise, he noticed a group of men huddled together, their voices hushed and their expressions filled with amusement. Lord Sinclair's curiosity piqued, and he decided to investigate.

Stepping into the ballroom, he scanned the room for Lady Angelina. But she was nowhere to be found. Instead, he saw Lady

Edwina, her smile strained as she engaged in conversation with a group of ladies. The atmosphere felt tense, as if a storm was brewing beneath the surface.

He joined the men and asked what caused them such amusement. Lord Bennett, drew him aside, and said, "It would seem, Lord Sinclair, that one of the ladies present has been caught in a rather compromising position with a stable lad! We are just trying to decide which one she is!" He laughed. "For if she would stoop so low for a commoner then what will she give to a lord!"

Lord Sinclair's stomach dropped. That was why the atmosphere was so tense. But it would seem that Lady Angelina hadn't been accused directly. Who the devil had found out?

His eyes narrowed in suspicion. He needed to speak with Angelina at once. He retraced his steps, his instincts leading him back towards the parlour. He had a feeling that she would be somewhere quiet, out of the limelight and away from further gossip.

As he entered the parlour, he found her standing alone, her posture guarded and her eyes filled with a mix of confusion and hurt. His heart sank at the sight of her, realizing the hurt she must be feeling.

"Lady Angelina," Lord Sinclair called out softly, his voice laced with concern. "Are you alright? I have been searching for you."

Lady Angelina turned to face him, her eyes shining with unshed tears. "Lord Sinclair," she whispered, her voice trembling with vulnerability. "I want to go home."

He rubbed his forehead, "What happened?"

"Lady Edwina has somehow found out about my - my indiscretion and she was taking immense delight in telling the other women but thankfully she didn't mention my name. I think she was about to reveal it but Lady Millicent intervened."

Lord Sinclair's heart clenched at Lady Angelina's words. He had suspected Lady Edwina's intentions, but now it was clear that she had indeed intended to spread gossip and isolate Lady Angelina.

Taking a step closer, Lord Sinclair reached out and gently grasped her hand. "Lady Angelina, please believe me when I say that not everyone sees you as Lady Edwina does. Your past does not define you, and I am here to support you."

Tears spilled down Lady Angelina's cheeks as she looked up at him, her eyes filled with a mix of gratitude and vulnerability. "Thank you," she whispered.

With a sense of determination, Lord Sinclair led Lady Angelina away from the parlour, away from the whispering tongues and judgmental looks. They walked through the grand hallway, leaving behind the toxicity of Lady Edwina's gathering.

As they stepped out into the cool night air, he assisted Lady Angelina into the carriage and once settled, told her that he would be back in a moment to join her.

Closing the carriage door, he turned his stern gaze towards the house. Now to deal with Lady Edwina and her abominable behaviour.

Chapter 7

Lady Edwina's gaze softened when she saw Lord Sinclair striding towards her across the ballroom. Perhaps he was going to ask her to dance. She smiled eagerly in anticipation. But as he drew nearer her smile began to falter for she could see that a dance was furthermost from his mind. His expression was quite foreboding.

Oh, dear. Was it directed at her?

He reached her side and placing his hand on her elbow, said, "A word if you please, Lady Edwina."

She immediately knew something was wrong and it could only have to do with Lady Angelina. Perhaps the chit had told lies about her?

Before she could say a word, she found Lord Sinclair was moving her swiftly towards the door. She wanted to dig her heels in but what scandal that would create. So smiling brilliantly at her guests, she made out she was going willingly.

She soon found herself in the parlour, alone with the very intimidating Lord Sinclair.

"Is there something wrong, Lord Sinclair?" she asked imperiously.

"You know very well what's wrong. You have been spreading unnecessary gossip."

"Whatever do you mean?" Her face flushed guiltily.

"I don't know how you found out, but Lady Angelina tells me you spoke about her indiscretion with the stable boy. Don't bother denying it. I would just like to know what you thought to gain by it - apart from ruining her reputation?"

"Oh, so you knew about it?"

He nodded.

"Yet you still had her live under your roof? Really, Lord Sinclair, whatever were you thinking?" She placed her hand on his arm, "I know it may seem harsh, Lord Sinclair, but sometimes the truth must be revealed in order for healing to begin. Lady Angelina needs to face the consequences of her actions if she is to grow and change. I was merely helping her."

Lord Sinclair raised an eyebrow. Lady Edwina's actions were bold, and her blatant disregard for others was obvious. She was so selfish and self-obsessed that she would do anything for her own gain.

"So you don't see anything wrong in what you did?" he queried.

He saw a flicker of uncertainty in her eyes but then she quickly hid it, "No! Of course not. Lady Angelina cannot hope to find a suitable match amongst the gentry now she has been spoiled. I do think that you should send her back to her parents house, Lord Sinclair. Rid yourself of the chit before your own reputation becomes sullied." She eyed him slyly. "One cannot stop gossiping tongues."

"I see."

He moved his arm so her hand dropped back to her side. Her true colours were finally showing and his previous misgivings about her now proved to be correct.

"I will take my leave and please do not presume to visit Withdean. If you do, I will give strict instructions that you are to be dismissed from the premises."

He turned around and strode out of the room, her voice echoing in his ears. "But Lord Sinclair... you cannot mean...!"

He didn't hear the rest. He wasn't interested. There was only one woman that he wanted to see now and that was Lady Angelina. Only time would reveal the true impact of Lady Edwina's whispered gossip about her. Although she hadn't mentioned her name yet, he knew she would at some point. She was too nasty to do otherwise.

Stepping into the plush carriage, Lord Sinclair's gaze fell upon Lady Angelina, her delicate frame trembling with silent sobs. She looked up at him with sorrowful eyes and it was all he could do not to gather her into his arms and protect her. But she wasn't his to protect as yet. Not in the way he wished.

Suppressing his own desires, he extended a hand towards her, a silent gesture of support and solace. With a gentle touch, he intertwined their fingers and smiling weakly, she leaned against his shoulder, seeking refuge in his unwavering strength.

As the carriage door closed, Lord Sinclair's cane tapped rhythmically against the carriage roof - a discreet signal to the driver to set the carriage in motion towards the sanctuary of home.

The morning sun cast a soft glow through the curtains as Lady Angelina slowly stirred from her slumber. As she opened her eyes, the events of the previous night flooded her mind and she closed her eyes again, groaning.

What had started out as a lovely evening had ended up being anything but. Lady Edwina had seen to that!

She sat up in bed, her thoughts swirling with a mix of emotions. Lady Edwina's actions had been calculated, an attempt to tarnish her reputation and undermine her potential connection with Lord Sinclair. But in her pursuit of power and jealousy, Lady Edwina had inadvertently pushed Lord Sinclair further away. Good!

Rising from the bed, she made her way to the vanity, gazing at her reflection in the mirror. Thankfully the tears she had shed last night hadn't left her with puffy eyes.

She didn't feel so bad today. Lord Sinclair's strength had given her a sense of resilience, not defeat. She wasn't going to let Lady Edwina's actions define her. Instead, she would rise above the gossip and get on with her life as usual.

Her thoughts turned to Lord Sinclair. She couldn't help but wonder how he had reacted to Lady Edwina's attempt to tarnish her reputation. Once he had settled her inside the carriage last night, he had strode back inside with purpose. Had he scolded her publicly? Had he spanked her?

The thought sent a ripple of excitement through her. Now *that* she would have liked to witness! The imperious Lady Edwina having her skirts lifted and hearing her wails echo across the dance floor. That would truly give her guests something to talk about.

Determined to find answers, Lady Angelina rang the bell for her maid and was soon washed and dressed. She chose an elegant gown with a pale blue bodice and cream skirt. A matching ribbon in her hair and she was ready to face Lord Sinclair.

"Is Lord Sinclair in the dining hall?" she asked Maude.

"Yes, m'lady, he arrived just before I came to assist you."

"He should still be there then." She strode to the door. "I will take my breakfast with Lord Sinclair this morning so don't worry about bringing anything to my room."

She arrived at the breakfast table to see Lord Sinclair reading the morning tabloid, eating a piece of buttered toast.

Their eyes met and she smiled demurely. "Good morning, my lord."

He folded the paper up and put it aside. "Good morning, Lady Angelina. It is unusual to see you here. I know you usually prefer to take your breakfast in your chambers."

"I wanted to speak with you about last night and as my lessons begin at nine, this is my only opportunity until the afternoon."

"Ah, I see." He looked at her carefully, "Are you recovered from your ordeal?"

She nodded. "Yes and I wanted to thank you for your help last night. I think if you hadn't been there to comfort me I would have fallen apart. Lady Edwina dislikes me to the point of trying to ruin me. I don't ever want to see her again!"

"No, in that we are in agreement. Unless she sends me a lengthy apology she won't step one foot inside this house."

Angelina reached for a piece of toast and began slathering it with butter. One of the servants poured her a cup of tea and placed it next to her.

"Did you speak with Lady Edwina just before we left?" Angelina asked, "I noticed you went back inside the house."

He nodded, "Yes. She is in no doubt as to how I feel."

Angelina looked at him from beneath her lashes and felt compelled to ask, "Did you spank her?" She said it low and quickly so the servants couldn't hear.

He leaned forward and his eyes intense, "No, that I keep solely for misbehaving little rebels who think to thwart my authority!"

Lady Angelina caught her breath, her eyes widening as she took in his meaning. She couldn't help the feeling of desire that shot through her, not only at the stern tone to his voice but his dark eyes that seemed to see into her very soul.

Lowering her lashes, she felt her cheeks grow red and quickly took a sip of tea to calm herself down. No man had ever made her feel this way and the thought of leaving him didn't bear thinking about.

She glanced up at him again and found he was staring at her but his eyes had softened somewhat. "I have a surprise for you," he said, "but it won't be until lunchtime. I trust you are able to take your lessons this morning with Miss Preston? After last night's ordeal I will understand if you need time to recover."

"No. I am determined to progress." she looked at him impishly, "but what is the surprise?"

He smiled, "I'm not going to tell you. Good things come to those who wait, my lady."

She pouted and rolled her eyes. "Very well."

She heard him laugh, a low rumble in his chest and she gave him a sideways glance. It was nice to see another side to him rather than the stern, unyielding lord she had first met. And when he smiled he was even more handsome if that were possible.

"You had better hurry, my lady. You know what happens if you are late for lessons!"

Angelina's eyes widened. Turning her attention to her breakfast she took a big bite of toast, a sip of tea and then excusing herself, quickly dashed off to the music room. Lord Sinclair's threat ringing in her ears.

Angelina's morning was consumed by the strict teachings of Miss Preston. Under her watchful eye, she practiced the art of walking with grace, maintaining proper posture, and executing the perfect curtsy.

As the lessons came to a close, Angelina couldn't help but feel a sense of exhaustion mingled with a newfound appreciation for the importance of poise and refinement. She retreated to her chambers, craving a moment of respite and a light lunch to replenish her energy. She was also dying to know what Lord Sinclair's surprise was!

Upon entering her chambers, her eyes widened in shock. There, standing in the room with a warm smile on her face, was Amy, her dear maid.

"Amy!" She exclaimed, her voice filled with genuine happiness. "You're back! How I have missed you!"

Tears glistened in Amy's eyes as she stepped forward, embracing Angelina in a warm hug. "Oh, m'lady, I have missed you terribly as well," she whispered. "I'm so grateful to be back in your service."

Angelina pulled away slightly, her hands grasping Amy's shoulders as she looked into her eyes. "Amy, I must apologize for the misunderstanding that led to your dismissal. It was a mistake, and I should have fought harder to ensure your place by my side. I did try but Lord Sinclair was so cross that he just wouldn't listen!"

Amy's eyes filled with understanding, a gentle smile gracing her lips. "M'lady, there is no need for apologies. I was just as much to blame as you. It was unfortunate that we were caught but now I am simply grateful for the opportunity to serve you once again."

A sense of gratitude washed over Angelina as she realized the depth of Amy's loyalty and forgiveness. She knew that she was fortunate to have such a devoted maid. With Amy's return, she could once again count on her unwavering support, not only as a maid but as a confidante and friend. Only this time perhaps they would try and stay out of trouble.

As they sat down for a light lunch, they both caught up on the events that had transpired during their time apart. In the midst of their conversation, Angelina couldn't help but wonder about the circumstances that had led to Amy's rehiring. She was obviously Lord Sinclair's surprise that he had informed her about but what had made him change his mind?

"Amy," Angelina began, her voice filled with curiosity. "I must know, how did you come to be rehired? And why was I not informed of this until today?"

Amy's expression turned sheepish, a hint of mischief twinkling in her eyes. "My Lady, it seems that Lord Sinclair took it upon himself to rectify the situation. He came to see me in person and said that because of the impact it had on you, he insisted that I should be reinstated as your maid. He did tell me that I must behave with more decorum."

Angelina sniggered, "That makes two of us!"

Amy laughed back, "Yes, I think perhaps we shall have to be more careful." She paused, remembering her conversation, "It was nice to see that Lord Sinclair wanted nothing more than to see you happy and well taken care of."

A surge of warmth flooded Angelina's heart. It was yet another testament to his character. He may be strict but he was proving to be a very fair man. How nice that he had gone to such lengths to ensure her happiness. She immediately felt contrite for the trouble she had caused him during her stay.

As Angelina and Amy continued their lunch, their conversation filled with laughter and shared memories, Angelina couldn't help but feel a sense of contentment wash over her. With Amy's return, a trusted confidante by her side, and Lord Sinclair's unwavering support, she knew that she was surrounded by the love and loyalty of those who truly cared for her.

— ⦿ —

Angelina had been at Withdean Manor for a whole month and she could honestly say that she had never experienced such a range of emotions. When she had arrived, she had been full of frustration and anger, then she had been exposed to Lady Edwina's toxic gossip and now she felt a sense of belonging.

What a tumultuous month it had been!

A wave of sadness crept over her as she realised that soon she would be leaving. She had become used to living at Withdean and the thought of returning to her own home wasn't appealing. She liked looking at the handsome Lord Sinclair. He had seemed so formidable in the beginning and in all truth, he surely had been, but now she had seen a softer more human side to him, it made the break even harder.

She laughed softly to herself. She had fallen in love with him. That was the plain and simple truth. She could deny her feelings no longer. He excited her. He was a man that one couldn't forget. His strength of character, his moral compass - it just set her heart fluttering and her pulse racing. No, leaving Withdean wasn't something she wanted to contemplate.

That evening, the dinner conversation had flowed pleasantly as always in Lord Sinclair's company. As they retired for coffee in the parlour, she gazed out at the rolling pastures and woods surrounding the estate.

"My lord, would it be possible to use one of your horses tomorrow? A gentle ride would do me a world of good and I haven't ridden in ages. Well, since I came here to be truthful."

Lord Sinclair smiled back warmly. "I see no reason why not. Just ensure you stay within the estate."

The next afternoon, Angelina made her way down to the stables. The stablehand had readied a beautiful chestnut mare, well-mannered but full of spirit.

"What's her name?" Angelina asked, stroking the velvety soft nose.

"Merry."

"Ah, it suits her!" She hoisted herself into the saddle and urged the mare out of the courtyard and then into a light canter towards the rolling pastures. With the wind in her hair, she felt truly free - she often rode at home and realised how much she had missed it.

She cantered on until she reached an open field and with a light kick to Merry's flanks, she was galloping across the land, the rhythmic sound of hooves against the ground providing a sense of tranquility.

She stayed within the boundaries of Lord Sinclair's land, as he had requested, relishing the opportunity to explore the vast estate.

As she rode further into the countryside, her thoughts drifted away from the troubles that had plagued her in recent days. The true beauty of nature was a welcome respite from the chaos that Lady Edwina had brought into her life.

As she rounded a bend in the path, however, she came face to face with none other than Lady Edwina herself, who appeared equally surprised by the encounter. The tension between them was palpable, an unspoken rivalry simmering beneath the surface.

Lady Edwina's eyes narrowed, her voice laced with disdain. "Lady Angelina, whatever are you doing here?"

"What does it look like I'm doing?" Angelina retorted. "And more to the point - what are you doing on Lord Sinclair's land?"

"I always ride here and it is you who is encroaching upon what is rightfully mine. Lord Sinclair's affections were meant for me, and yet you seek to capture his heart."

Angelina, determined not to let Lady Edwina's words affect her, replied calmly, "Lady Edwina, Lord Sinclair's heart is not an object to be claimed. It belongs to whomever he chooses."

Enraged by Angelina's composed response, Lady Edwina's face twisted with anger. She spurred her horse forward, attempting to intimidate her rival. The horses reared up, their hooves clashing as they tried to avoid each other.

In the midst of the commotion, Lady Edwina lost control of her horse and was thrown off, landing with a thud on the ground. Panic gripped Angelina. She didn't like the woman but she wished no harm on her. Settling her horse, she swiftly dismounted and rushed to Lady Edwina's side.

"Lady Edwina, are you alright?" Lady Angelina asked, her voice filled with genuine concern.

Lady Edwina winced in pain, clutching her arm. "You did this! You deliberately caused my fall! You wanted to get rid of me, didn't you?"

Angelina's eyes widened in disbelief. "Don't talk such nonsense! I would never wish harm upon anyone. This was a mere accident which you yourself caused!"

Angelina helped Lady Edwina to her feet and quickly realised that she was just trying to blame her for something that she herself had caused. Would she stop at nothing to get her in trouble with Lord Sinclair?

Lady Edwina brushed her skirts down and pulled a face when she saw mud on the hem of her riding habit. "Look what you've done!"

Angelina rolled her eyes, trying to quell her temper, "Don't blame me for your actions! I didn't cause your fall, you did. I'm truly sorry that this accident occurred, but I will not bear the blame for something beyond my control."

Lady Edwina, still seething with anger, brushed off her attempts at explanation. She mounted her horse, casting one final glare in her direction before riding off, leaving Angelina to contemplate the consequences of their clash. The woman was so obsessed with Lord Sinclair that she wondered if she would ever cease trying to ensnare him.

With a heavy sigh, she mounted her horse once again, deciding to continue her ride and find solace in the beauty of the countryside. She knew that she couldn't let Lady Edwina's anger consume her own spirit. Instead, she would focus on herself and rise above her provocation... for now!

Chapter 8

Angelina returned from her ride and sought solace in her chambers. Staring out of the window, with her arms folded across her chest, she wondered why Lady Edwina couldn't just accept that Lord Sinclair wasn't interested in her? And what had given her leave to think that she herself was a rival.

She admitted that she was quite in love with him but as to whether it was reciprocated, she knew not. Maybe Lady Edwina knew something she didn't?

Amy arrived with a tray of tea and small pastries, placing it on the main table. Angelina swiftly told her to take a seat so she could confide in her, telling her everything that had happened down to the last detail.

Amy listened attentively, her eyes widening as Angelina relayed the events to her. "M'lady, we cannot let Lady Edwina's jealousy and deceit continue to harm you. We must devise a plan, a way to expose her true nature so that everyone can see her for who she truly is."

A mischievous smile curled on Lady Angelina's lips as an idea started to form in her mind. "What if we use Lady Edwina's own games against her? I can be equally as cunning and I think I know a way to make her squirm!"

Amy's eyes sparkled with intrigue. "Tell me your plan, m'lady, and maybe I can help."

Two days later, Lord Sinclair received an invitation to an afternoon tea party hosted by one of his acquaintances, Lord Alexander. He showed Angelina the invite when they sat down to dinner and her heart skipped a beat when she saw that Lady Edwina's name was also on the guest list. She knew that this event presented the perfect opportunity to set their plan in motion. Her eyes sparkled wickedly and she smiled.

"Why do you smile so, Lady Angelina?" Lord Sinclair asked her, eyeing her speculatively.

"Oh, I am just excited to be invited. It will be fun."

He continued staring at her, and she knew he was trying to ascertain whether or not she was up to no good. So she continued smiling and reaching for her spoon, took a delicate mouthful of soup, keeping her eyes averted. He was so astute that one look into her eyes and he would know she had devious plans.

She heard him give a suspicious, "hmmm" before he too, turned his attention to the first course.

Thankfully, he hadn't pursued his suspicions. That was the last thing she needed!

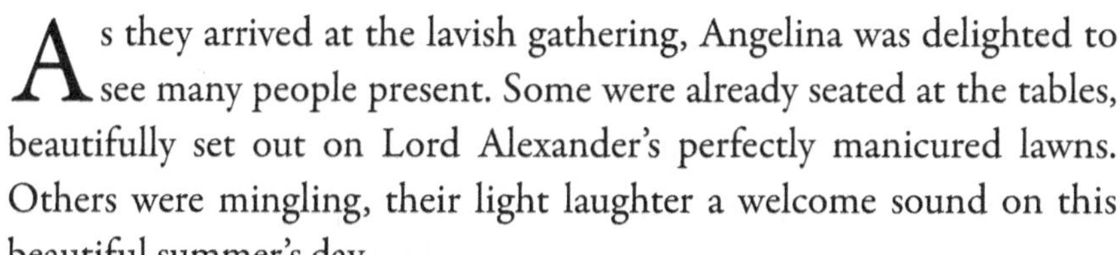

As they arrived at the lavish gathering, Angelina was delighted to see many people present. Some were already seated at the tables, beautifully set out on Lord Alexander's perfectly manicured lawns. Others were mingling, their light laughter a welcome sound on this beautiful summer's day.

Lord Sinclair introduced her to some of his friends and business acquaintances. She curtseyed prettily and assessed them one by one, searching for the perfect candidate to play a crucial role in her scheme. So far, only one man seemed suitable, Lord Archie. He wasn't conventionally attractive, in fact he was very plain and he possessed an air of simplicity. She had seen him at Lady Edwina's soirée so knew he was already in her social circle. He might be perfect but she would wait awhile and see who else she was introduced to.

The man had to be a bit gullible and easy to manipulate and most of the men present were neither.

Lord Sinclair handed her a glass of sparkling champagne. "Are you looking for someone in particular, my lady? You seem a little preoccupied if you don't mind me saying." He lowered his voice slightly, "I hope you're not worried about Lady Edwina?"

"Oh, no. Not at all." She should be more worried about me, she thought quietly to herself, hiding a smirk. "I have been humiliated enough by her wicked tongue. I won't let it happen again. After all, it is just her word against mine."

He smiled, "I am glad to hear it. Now, follow me, I have found a table for us and my good friend, Lady Millicent is keeping our seats for us. I think you met her recently, at Lady Edwina's soirée."

A little while later, Lord Sinclair watched Angelina as she spoke with Lady Millicent. They had met briefly before but this time, as he had predicted, they had immediately taken to one another and had hardly stopped talking since. He smiled indulgently, enjoying seeing his ward carrying herself with such dignity and decorum. Lady Millicent was a calming influence and her many years of experience meant she could offer advice on practically any subject.

He looked up to find Lord Alexander with his finger raised to catch his attention, so he excused himself from the table, leaving the two women to continue their conversation.

Halfway across the lawns, he was accosted by Lady Edwina. He tensed and regarded her with steely eyes.

"Lord Sinclair, how lovely to see you here." She lowered her lashes for a moment and then said, "I was hoping we could speak with one another. I wish to apologise for my behaviour the other night. I have had time to reflect and I understand your displeasure. I realise now that my plan to embarrass Lady Angelina was not befitting of a lady. I allowed my anger and frustration to cloud my judgment, and for that, I am truly sorry." She looked at him but in her eyes he saw no sincerity, only a need for him to believe her.

Lord Sinclair sighed and then said, "Lady Edwina, your behaviour that night was unforgivable. Revenge and vindictiveness do not align with the kindness and grace that I used to admire in you." His tone was brusque and unyielding.

"Used to?" She angled her head, a look of alarm crossing her face. "You mean you do not admire me now?"

"I will not lie to you. I neither admire you or detest you. But I no longer wish to be in your company. Forgive me, but I speak plainly."

He bowed eloquently and left her gaping after him. If she hadn't got the message last time they spoke, then she cannot have missed it now.

Dismissing the selfish woman from his thoughts, he continued his route towards Lord Alexander.

Left alone, Lady Millicent patted Angelina's hand and said, "I hope you don't mind me mentioning this, but now we are alone, I want to tell you to pay no heed to idle gossip."

Her smile was warm, her eyes filled with empathy.

"Oh! You mean..."

Lady Millicent's expression softened, her gentle gaze conveying understanding and reassurance. "My dear Lady Angelina, I understand the pain and anxiety that come with society's whispers. I think we have all experienced it at one time or another. But let me assure you, gossip blows over like the wind, and it is our strength and resilience that ultimately defines us."

Angelina's eyes widened in surprise, not expecting such a revelation from the esteemed Lady Millicent. "You too, Lady Millicent? I had no idea."

A soft chuckle escaped Lady Millicent's lips. "Oh, my dear, if only you knew the secrets hidden behind the polished veneer of the upper echelons of society. We have all made mistakes, encountered moments of indiscretion, and faced the judgment of our peers. But it is in how we carry ourselves and rise above the gossip that truly matters."

Angelina's shoulders relaxed as she absorbed Lady Millicent's words of wisdom. "Thank you, Lady Millicent. Your words mean so very much to me."

Lady Millicent offered a comforting smile. "I am always nearby if you ever need a shoulder to cry on. Just know that this momentary stumble will not define you."

Angelina heard the sincerity in her voice and it heartened her. But it didn't stop her desire to get her revenge on Lady Edwina. Oh no, indeed.

Excusing herself, she decided to wander amongst the guests and see if she could find the man to unwittingly help her exact vengeance on the odious woman.

A little while later and after carefully assessing the men present, she finally determined that Lord Archie was the sole individual who met her requirements. He was seated, engrossed in stroking one of Lord Alexander's dogs, and happened to be alone. How fortunate!

Approaching him with a friendly smile, she said, "Lord Archie, how lovely to see you here."

He glanced up, his face brightening with a wide smile. "Lady Angelina." Swiftly rising to his feet, he offered her a polite bow.

Angelina quickly engaged in a brief, courteous conversation before addressing the true purpose of her visit. Lowering her voice, she continued, "My lord, there is something of importance I need to inform you about. It is a delicate matter, but one I believe you should be aware of."

"Oh?" He tilted his head. "This sounds rather intriguing."

"It concerns Lady Edwina. She has confided in me numerous times about her admiration for you."

He drew in a sharp breath. "She has?"

Angelina nodded. "She secretly longs for your attention, and as her friend and confidante, I believe it is time for you to know. If you share similar sentiments, I think you should act upon your feelings. Disregard any rejections she may present, as they are merely a façade. Lady Edwina is teasing you, but deep down, she genuinely holds affection for you."

Lord Archie's eyes widened in surprise and he seemed unsure of how to respond to her unexpected revelation. "You are certain of this, Lady Angelina? I have always admired her for her grace and charm but I never dared to hope she would return my feelings."

Grace and charm be damned, Angelina thought, thinking of the harridan in question. More like, anger and vitriol!

She looked at Lord Archie's face and felt a slight pang of guilt for her actions but then remembered why she was doing this in the first place. Revenge!

"Truly, Lord Archie, she most definitely has a secret longing for you."

Angelina watched him carefully, hoping he was going to take the bait. And indeed he did. Squaring his shoulders, he rubbed his hands together and said, "Well then, I must go and speak to the dear lady at once!"

"Please don't tell her that it was I that told you. She would be very cross that I had said anything, but you see," she clasped her hands together over her heart, "I am a lady who believes in true love and I think you two would make the most perfect couple."

He nodded, his determination clear to see. "Fear not, Lady Angelina. Your secret is safe with me!"

Angelina watched him go and smiled slyly. Oh yes, Lady Edwina, let's see how you cope with a bit of drama!

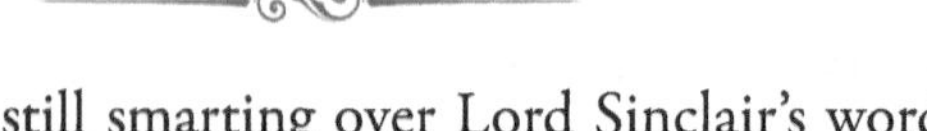

Lady Edwina was still smarting over Lord Sinclair's words. It was extremely rude of him not to accept her apology. Maybe Lady Angelina had put him up to it! That must be it. Before he'd met that little harlot he had always been full of admiration and respect for her. She had been so close to marriage and now it was not to be.

Her hand curled into a fist by her side and she knew such intense anger that for a moment she thought she would scream. But that would never do. Swallowing hard to calm herself down, she reached for a glass of champagne from one of the waiters and quickly took a gulp.

"Lady Edwina!" A voice said next to her. She looked around to find Lord Archie before her.

She gave him a tight lipped smile. The boring buffoon was the last person she wanted to talk to right at this moment. "Oh, Lord Archie, I didn't know you would be here today?"

"Neither did I. Lord Alexander saw me in town last night and kindly invited me. I am so very glad he did." His eyes took on a hint of familiarity and Lady Edwina immediately tensed, sensing something amiss. "If I may be so bold," he continued, "I would like to say that I have admired you from afar for quite some time now, Lady Edwina."

Oh dear, she thought, where is this going? She eyed him warily, waiting for him to continue.

"Your grace, intelligence, and wit have captivated my heart. I cannot deny the deepening affection I feel for you." He placed his hand over his heart and looked at her with longing.

Lady Edwina looked at him askance. "I beg your pardon, Lord Archie. Why do you speak to me in such a fashion? This is most alarming!"

Lord Archie's eyes widened with surprise, his features reflecting a mix of confusion and disappointment. But undeterred, he carried on, "Lady Edwina, I understand if my declaration catches you off guard but I cannot deny the admiration for you. Please, allow me the chance to prove my sincere intentions." He took one of her hands and kissed her knuckles, "I would respectfully request the opportunity to court you."

Lady Edwina, quickly pulled her hand away and looked around to see if anyone had noticed. This was all rather embarrassing.

"Lord Archie, you are mistaken if you believe I share any affection for you. Your advances are quite unwelcome, I can assure you."

Lord Archie remained steadfast, his voice unwavering. "Lady Edwina, forgive me if I refuse to accept your rejection but it has come to my attention that you reciprocate my feelings."

"Who on earth told you that?" she snapped. Her raised voice started to turn heads and within seconds, a few of her friends were listening in attentively. It was always interesting when Lady Edwina was riled.

Lord Archie took a step closer, his eyes filled with determination. "I will not reveal my source but I beseech you, Lady Edwina, to give me a chance. I am willing to prove myself worthy of your affections. I will do anything!"

"Desist this foolishness!" Her face was beginning to flush beet red at being the centre of such unwanted attention. "You are making a spectacle of yourself."

He suddenly seemed to become aware of how many people were staring at him and even his cheeks began to flame. With a muttered apology he stumbled away towards the house, a look of embarrassment on his face.

Lady Edwina stood still for a fleeting moment, her mind grappling with the revelation that Lord Archie believed she had feelings for him. The notion was preposterous! She had never entertained the idea of him as a potential suitor. In her eyes, he was far too ordinary, lacking the charm and stature befitting a lady of her means and social standing.

A furrow formed on her brow as she contemplated her next move. Just as she was about to turn away, a movement caught her attention. A glimpse of Lady Angelina's face beneath the shade of a large oak tree.

She was clearly gloating and she knew it was aimed solely at her. The glimmer of satisfaction dancing in her eyes was clear to see!

In that instant, Lady Edwina's intuition made a resolute connection, and she knew precisely who had sown the seed of this misconception within Lord Archie's mind.

A little while later, as the afternoon tea came to a close, the guests started to bid their farewells and depart in their waiting carriages, everyone agreeing that the event had been a resounding success. Even more so for Angelina who was extremely satisfied, to say the least. Her intricate plan had worked!

She had found the time to make amends with Lord Archie for she felt quite remorseful that she had put him in such a position. She had hurt his feelings and that wasn't a nice thing to do.

She had told him that she couldn't understand why Lady Edwina had reacted to his show of affection in such a manner and that perhaps it was because being in such a public area, she had felt compelled to hide her true feelings. With time, Lady Edwina could reflect on his proposal and perhaps he should call on her.

It had lifted his spirits and he had thanked her for her caring nature. His words made Angelina squirm a little for she was the instigator of the whole thing. But she was happy to see him with a happier disposition.

Sitting in the carriage opposite Lord Sinclair as the wheels began to trundle along the gravel drive towards home, she reflected on the evening. It had proved to be most entertaining!

His voice broke through her thoughts. "Lady Angelina, something happened this afternoon that was most troubling." His eyes were dark and unfathomable.

Angelina immediately tensed, "Oh?"

"I want to ask if you had any knowledge of Lady Edwina's embarrassing conversation with Lord Archie," he inquired, leveling his eyes on her.

Her eyes widened in surprise, her heart beginning to pound with apprehension. "I didn't hear it myself but I overheard others speaking about it. Why do you ask?" She tried to remain calm and indifferent but under his stern gaze, it was proving to be a difficult task.

He hesitated for a moment before revealing the truth. "Lady Edwina confided in me earlier today. She believes that you may have played a part in orchestrating the conversation, that you deliberately misled Lord Archie into thinking she had feelings for him."

Angelina's breath caught in her throat. "I would never stoop to such deceitful tactics, Lord Sinclair. I would never intentionally harm Lady Edwina in such a manner." She fiddled nervously with the folds of her skirts. "Besides, you know her character. She is mean and wouldn't hesitate to try and get someone into trouble!"

"That much is true but neither would you."

"I wouldn't!" She raised her chin, starting to get annoyed.

"Of course you wouldn't." His eyes grew dark. "Or so I thought, until I spoke to Lord Archie himself and he told me the truth."

"Whatever he said isn't true!" Angelina said quickly.

He leaned forward and took her hand. "I've known Lord Archie for years and I know him to be honest and reputable. You, however, are proving to be anything but!"

Angelina gasped and tried to pull her hand out of his but he held it firm.

"Why did you do it? Why did you deliberately make a fool of them? This behaviour is most unbecoming." His lips thinned. "Have you learned nothing in the past few weeks?"

"Well, of course I have."

"I fear you have not." He looked down at her hand and then to her utter dismay, said, "But you will learn. As soon as we arrive home, we are going to visit the study and you know what that means, don't you?"

Her breathing became erratic and she went to speak but he raised his finger. "Not another word until we are home."

Angelina leaned back against her seat and thrust her bottom lip out angrily. Once again she was in trouble with the formidable Lord Sinclair! Would she ever learn?

Chapter 9

As the carriage came to a stop outside Withdean Manor, Lord Sinclair opened the door and offered his hand to Angelina. His face was set and unmoving.

She took his hand tentatively and stepped out onto the gravel. Oh, lord, she was in so much trouble!

He kept hold of her hand and steered her up the wide stone steps into the house. She felt so small beside him and couldn't help the nervous tremour that rippled through her at her impending punishment.

Her sense of elation earlier at having embarrassed Lady Edwina had promptly backfired and here she was again, experiencing Lord Sinclair's wrath. She should have known better.

Opening the door to the study, he ushered her in and closed it firmly behind them. The atmosphere grew tense as Lord Sinclair's frustration simmered beneath the surface. Angelina could sense his annoyance, her heart sinking with a mix of guilt and apprehension. She hadn't anticipated the outcome of her actions and truly thought she could get away with her plan, but now, here she was, facing the consequences.

Lord Sinclair, his expression stern, picked up a wooden chair and placed it in the centre of the room. "Come here."

Her heart skipped a beat as she tried to calm her nerves and unwittingly she took a step backwards. She thought about running out of the room but knew he would soon catch her and then things might get even worse.

He arched an eyebrow. "Are you going to come here, or am I going to have to come and get you? You know what the consequences will be if I have to come and get you, don't you?"

Angelina's chest was heaving, and she fiddled nervously with her hands. "Please, Lord Sinclair, I won't even think of doing anything like that again! I promise."

"I won't ask again." He warned her.

She steeled her nerves and reluctantly did as he asked, placing herself in front of his hard thighs. Oh, lord, this was going to hurt!

Lord Sinclair placed his hand on her arm and moved her to his side, drawing her down onto his lap. She closed her eyes tightly, mortified that she was again in such an intimate position.

Swiftly, he pulled up her dress and parting her bloomers, he settled his large hand on one of her buttocks. His touch was electric and even though Angelina knew it was going to hurt, she couldn't help the thrill that surged through her slender body.

"It pains me that I have to do this but you leave me no choice." He said, his deep voice filling her senses.

He began lightly spanking her bottom and then increased in tempo, alternating between both cheeks until Angelina was writhing in pain as the stinging became too much to bear.

"Ouch! Please Lord Sinclair, no more!"

She tried to wriggle backwards off his lap, but Lord Sinclair just heaved her further forward until her hands touched the ground. He gave her five more hefty swats that left her panting to cope with the pain and her bottom throbbing unbearably.

With his hand still lying on her tender skin, he scolded her further, "I do hope you learn by this, my lady."

"I will, I will!"

"I am not so sure. Lady Edwina possesses a rather unfortunate character but that doesn't mean you have to stoop to her level. Do you understand?"

"Absolutely! It won't happen again!" Angelina nodded for all she was worth. It was a little disconcerting having a conversation with the esteemed lord, whilst draped over his lap with her bottom bare. His touch was doing all sorts of things to her emotions and it was hard to concentrate on what he was saying.

As she was just beginning to think her punishment was over, she felt the cold, hard surface of wood against her bottom, resting on both cheeks.

She gasped and tried to pull herself off his lap. "Lord Sinclair! What do you do?"

"Stay still!" He tapped her buttocks with the wooden implement and said, "I am going to give you five swats with this ruler and you can think yourself lucky that's all I am giving you!"

She knew by the tone of his voice he was deadly serious, but even so, she didn't want any more punishment and certainly not the hard contact of a wooden ruler! She was darned if she was going to submit to it!

She tried to struggle again, but found her whole body moving forward as Lord Sinclair brought the ruler crashing down onto both buttocks.

She shrieked in pain and clenched her bottom to try and stop further strikes, but he carried on regardless, the ruler swinging down again and again onto her bright red buttocks.

"Ow! Oh!" Lord it was painful!

Lord Sinclair landed the final swat on the perfect little derriere draped across his lap. Angelina's bottom bore the marks of her punishment and no doubt, she wouldn't be sitting very comfortably for a few days.

But it served her right.

One way or another, he would teach her to amend her ways. She was far too headstrong and reckless. He still couldn't quite believe the mischief she had created that day.

He replaced the ruler on the desk and couldn't help but trace the red impact mark on her hot bottom. He heard her sharp intake of breath and wondered if it was from pain or arousal. He certainly knew how he felt.

Reluctantly, he pulled her bloomers together and pulled her skirts back down to cover her bottom. He drew her up from his lap and stood her before him, keeping her close by holding both her hands.

Her bottom lip was thrust out and she was refusing to look at him, keeping her gaze lowered.

"I hope you understand why I just punished you?" He said, his thumbs circling the back of her hands.

Angelina spoke, her voice barely above a whisper. "I do understand. I acted impulsively and should have known better, my lord."

Lord Sinclair sighed, wondering if she was truly regretful of her actions or would quite happily do the same thing again if someone thwarted her!

"It is important to remember that sometimes it is better to ignore the actions of others. Rise above their behaviour and show them how to act with decorum."

Lady Angelina's shot to his and in their blue depths, he yet saw a hint of defiance, "Even if they have done something atrocious?"

"Yes."

She snorted softly, clearly in disagreement so he quickly decided other tactics were needed to finish off her punishment. "Lady Angelina, in light of your actions today, I believe it would be best for you to retire to your chambers without dinner tonight. This will give you time to reflect upon your actions and the impact they have had on those around you."

Her eyes widened in surprise, "No dinner!"

He shook his head.

"But that's not fair! Haven't you punished me enough?" She stomped her foot on the floor and he raised an eyebrow.

"Continue in that vein and I will take the cane to your backside!" he said sharply.

She gasped and immediately looked contrite.

He let go of her hands and standing up, he ushered her towards the door, "Now, you are to go directly to your chambers." He opened the thick wooden door, "No dallying, no dithering, straight to bed!"

With that last word of warning, he watched her go, her back straight, her small chin raised in the air and a look of resigned indignation on her face. She would learn, one way or another.

As she lay in bed that night, her stomach empty and her heart heavy, Angelina knew that she had much to atone for. In the silence of her solitude, she resolved to make things right with Lord Sinclair. She was determined to try to become a little less hot-headed but it wasn't going to be easy!

People like Lady Edwina were trouble makers and in her humble opinion, needed taking down a peg or two. Lord Sinclair's suggestion to ignore them just wasn't in her repertoire.

Even though she now sported a sore backside, it had been worth it to see Lady Edwina squirm so. She sniggered to herself, remembering the events of the day.

Well, one thing was certain, she would have to amend her ways but only to become more careful and avoid Lord Sinclair's wrath. She reached down a hand and ran her fingers over the small raised welts on her soft skin. It was still tender.

But there was something about his dominance that she found thrilling. Having to answer for her actions and be held accountable was rather exciting. A battle of wills.

And so, she closed her eyes, her mind filled with the image of the handsome lord and wondering what the next few days would bring.

Several days passed by, and Angelina, ever determined, made a conscientious effort to conduct herself with utmost propriety. She managed to appear attentive as she listened to lessons in the morning from the rather tedious Miss Preston and in the afternoons, under Lord Sinclair's guidance, she felt that had truly improved.

She had become quite used to living at Withdean Manor and knew that when the time came to leave, it would indeed be with a heavy heart.

She finished her lunch and pushed the plate away, just as Amy popped her head around the door. "Have you finished, m'lady?"

"Yes, Amy. Come in."

She walked in and as she began to clear the plates back onto the tray, she said. "Lord Sinclair told me to tell you that your father has arrived."

Angelina looked up shocked, "My father?"

"Yes, he arrived a few minutes ago but Lord Sinclair said to finish your lunch before coming down."

Angelina's heart fluttered with a mix of excitement and sadness. Was he here to take her home?

It had been over a month since Lord Sinclair had taken her under his guardianship, and in that time, she had learned valuable lessons and experienced a journey of self-discovery. However, the prospect of returning home was bittersweet, for it meant leaving Lord Sinclair behind.

As she made her way to the parlour to greet her father, her mind raced with conflicting emotions. She knew deep down that Lord Sinclair's guidance and instruction had been instrumental in her growth, and part of her wished she could stay by his side, continuing to learn from his wisdom and presence. Even if it meant receiving a spanking or two.

When she entered the parlour, she found her father alone, a warm smile on his face. "Angelina, my dear, you look radiant."

She walked up to him and kissed him on the cheek, "Papa, how lovely to see you."

"I hope your time under Lord Sinclair's guardianship has been beneficial."

"Yes, Papa. I have learned so much during my time with him. He has imparted wisdom upon me and guided me in ways I never thought possible." She thought about going over his lap and how his spankings had certainly made her rethink her attitude. As for whether she learned from it, well, that was another matter!

Her father's eyes softened as he observed her. "I am pleased to hear that, Angelina. Lord Sinclair is a man of great character and knowledge and I can clearly see a change in you already. I believe putting you under his care was most definitely a good decision. Now, go and instruct your maid to pack your things and we will return home. Your mother is missing you dreadfully."

With a heavy heart, Angelina returned to her chambers and sat down on the bed. She was not only having to leave the beautiful manor, but also a person who had become dear to her. She wondered if Lord Sinclair felt the same way about her as she did about him. Had their time together forged a bond? Did he feel it too?

Amy came into the room and Angelina immediately saw the tears threatening to fall. "Oh, m'lady. I am going to miss you!"

Angelina quickly rushed over and hugged her. "I feel the same but I promise to come back and visit! I will insist that Lord Sinclair let you have time off so we can take tea together!"

"Oh, will you now?" A voice said from the doorway.

They both spun around to find Lord Sinclair leaning against the door frame. His eyes were intensely focused on Angelina.

"Amy, would you leave us for a moment." he said quietly.

When she had gone, Lord Sinclair walked over to Angelina. "I believe that I, too, will miss you, Lady Angelina." His eyes were dark and she sensed unspoken words.

Angelina blushed, "And I you, Lord Sinclair. You have taught me some important lessons on how to behave in society and I thank you for it."

She wanted to say more but she was his ward and he her guardian so it would be unseemly if she stepped outside those boundaries. She searched his face, drinking in every last detail for she had no idea when or if she would see him again.

"I will rejoin your father and await you in the drawing room."

She watched him go and wanted to say so much, but daren't. She knew this day would come and once had longed for it. Now she longed for the opposite.

In the carriage, as the wheels rolled along the path towards her home, Lady Angelina couldn't help but feel a sense of loss.

Her father sensed her melancholy. "You seem sad to leave, my dear."

Angelina smiled softly, "Yes. It has been quite an adventure, Papa. But I do feel stronger for it and I have learned my lesson as you hoped."

"I am very glad to hear that. I hope you now understand how your behaviour reflects upon our family name."

"Oh, yes, Lord Sinclair left me in no doubt as to how important it is to avoid any sort of scandal." She leaned forward and took her father's hand. "I am truly sorry for the trouble I caused, Papa. Will you forgive me?"

Her father turned to her, a knowing smile on his lips. "My dear, of course I shall. I can see that by taking you under his wing, Lord Sinclair has guided you with great care. You have learned so very much."

Angelina's heart lifted, happy to be out of her father's bad books.

As the carriage arrived at her family's estate, Angelina stepped out with a mixture of excitement and longing. She was eager to see her family but a part of her would always remain entwined with Lord Sinclair and the experience he had given her.

In her heart, Angelina held the hope that their paths would cross again. Sooner rather than later. She was already missing his handsome face and the undeniable attraction she felt for him.

Resigning herself to life without him, for now, she walked into the house to greet her mother, who was simply dying to know how her time had been spent with the rather austere Lord Sinclair.

Life settled back to normal and Angelina found her days filled with either horse riding, embroidery or reading book after book but no matter what she did, she couldn't get Lord Sinclair out of her mind. She had tried to but when she fell asleep at night, he was the man she dreamed of. When she awoke in the morning she would remember the intense dreams and feel such a sense of longing that she wanted to ride across the fields without stopping until she reached Withdean Manor.

One morning, as she sat in the elegant dining room at the breakfast table, her mother noticed her rather melancholy gaze and said, "Angelina, I cannot help but notice that you seem a bit downcast this morning. Perhaps a change of scenery would do you good. Why don't you and your sister take the carriage into town? Go to the boutique and treat yourselves to new dresses."

Angelina's eyes met her mother's, "Mama, what a wonderful idea! Susannah what do you think? A trip to town would do us both good."

Susannah grinned, "I would love it. Oh, thank you, mama!"

Lady Beatrice's smile widened, her eyes filled with warmth. "You are most welcome, my dears. It will do you both good to spend some time together. A simple change of scenery is good for the soul."

With eager excitement, Angelina and her sister, Susannah, made their way to the carriage, the anticipation of a new dress brightening their eyes. As they journeyed towards town, the gentle sway of the carriage offered a respite from the heaviness that had burdened Angelina's heart.

When they arrived in the bustling streets, they stepped out of the carriage right outside their favourite boutique and ventured inside.

Susannah was two years older than her but they had always got on exceptionally well. Yes, they had the odd argument but who didn't? But they were very like-minded.

Susannah picked up a rather hideous dress and with a straight face said, "Take this one, Angelina. I think it would rather suit you."

Angelina looked at her askance and then saw the devilish glint in her sister's eyes. "No, you have it. I wouldn't want to deprive you!"

They both burst out laughing and continued looking at the dresses and accessories. An hour later they had made several purchases. The dresses they had chosen needed alterations so wouldn't be ready for a few days but they had new hats, gloves and several pretty hairpins. All in all it was an afternoon well spent.

As they were standing talking at the counter, waiting for their purchases to be properly packaged, the bell above the door rang, signaling a new customer. Angelina looked over and her face fell immediately. It was Lady Edwina!

Their eyes met and neither smiled. Susannah sensing the tension in the air, looked from one to the other silently appraising the situation.

Lady Edwina breezed over and her eyes swept over Angelina with disdain. "Oh, I hadn't expected to find you here."

Angelina's eyes narrowed. "Likewise."

Lady Edwina's expression grew cold and she met Angelina's gaze with a calculating gleam in her eyes. "I have some news that may interest you. I am recently engaged."

"Oh?"

She held up her hand and showed her a large diamond ring. "It was a rather sudden proposal but when two hearts are joined then one cannot wait!"

Angelina looked at the rather ostentatious ring and politely asked, "And who is the lucky man?"

"Why can't you guess? It is Lord Sinclair of course!"

Lady Angelina's world shattered in an instant. Her heart sank, and a wave of disbelief washed over her. The joy that had filled her moments ago now turned to a deep ache of betrayal. She swayed slightly, her shock apparent.

Lady Edwina's lips curled into a smirk, her eyes filled with a malicious glint. "Oh, my dear, I can see you are upset. Perhaps you misunderstood Lord Sinclair's intentions? He and I have been courting for quite some time now and always had an understanding." She tittered into her hand, "But when he no longer had you to encumber him and take up his valuable time, he proposed straight away! I cannot tell you how delighted I was!"

Tears welled in Angelina's eyes as the weight of Lady Edwina's words settled upon her. The future she had envisioned with Lord Sinclair crumbled before her, replaced by a harsh reality she could scarcely comprehend.

In that moment, Angelina felt a mix of anger, heartbreak, and a profound sense of loss. The emotions were overwhelming, threatening to consume her.

Susannah sensed her dismay and quickly slid her arm through hers for support. "I think we should leave now, dearest. I will send Foster in to collect our packages." She nodded politely at Lady Edwina and steered Angelina to the exit. "Good afternoon to you, Lady Edwina."

Susannah didn't miss the flash of satisfaction in Lady Edwina's eyes or the evil glint that followed.

Angelina walked out of the boutique with a heavy heart. The yearning she had for Lord Sinclair had not been returned. She closed her eyes and a single tear ran down her face. The love she had for him was all for nothing.

Chapter 10

The carriage rolled along the country road, carrying Angelina and her sister, Susannah, back to their family estate. What had started out as such a lovely day, had quickly turned into one of abject misery.

Angelina brushed another tear from her cheek and stared out of the window. How could Lord Sinclair wish to marry such an odious woman? It certainly wasn't for her money because with his vast wealth, he had no need. Maybe it was for her status? Or maybe because she was older than Angelina, perhaps he found her more refined, more sophisticated.

She curled her hands into fists, frustrated, sad and angry all at the same time.

Susannah took her hand and tried to offer comfort, "Angelina, I can't bear seeing you upset like this. I don't know Lord Sinclair very well but is he worth getting upset over? If he has chosen Lady Edwina over you, perhaps he isn't very astute and not worthy of becoming your suitor? She doesn't seem very nice. I saw a nasty glint in her eye and took an instant dislike to the woman."

Angelina looked at her sharply, "A glint, you say?"

Susannah nodded, "Yes, a calculating look. I didn't imagine it either, it was plain to see."

"Then she could have been lying." Angelina reasoned, beginning to perk up. She wiped her tears away as she realised who she was dealing with. "She could have made the whole thing up!"

"Why would she do such a thing?"

"She considers me a rival so it would be the perfect way to get back at me. Why, I bet that ring wasn't even real." She concluded "Even if it was, it was far too gaudy a ring! Lord Sinclair would never give her anything so garish!"

Susannah reached out and squeezed her sister's hand, her voice filled with determination. "You are right. We cannot jump to conclusions, Angelina. Let us wait and see. Perhaps there is an explanation, a truth that has yet to be revealed."

— ❦ —

A *week later...*
Days turned into a week, and the weight of uncertainty settled upon Angelina's heart. She hadn't been able to find out any more information regarding Lord Sinclair's engagement to Lady Edwina. Which was odd in itself and heartened her no end. He was so prestigious that if it were true then everyone would be talking about it. And they weren't!

It still didn't stop her from thinking the worst.

She was sitting under a big oak tree, on the manicured lawns at the front of the house and was trying to read but it was no good, she just couldn't seem to focus on the words. Her mind was still in a whirl.

Lost in her own thoughts, her eyes wandered lazily across the landscape until a flicker of movement caught her attention at the end of the tree-lined drive.

Her heart skipped a beat as she recognized the figure on horseback approaching. It was the very man she couldn't stop thinking about - Lord Sinclair.

A surge of anticipation coursed through her veins, tingling with a mixture of curiosity and delight. Had he come to visit her? Had he come to announce his engagement to the harpy?

As he gracefully dismounted and gave his horse over to the care of a stable hand, Angelina watched him intently to see where he would go.

Had he seen her sitting on the lawn? He couldn't very well miss her as her blanket was spread out. She stood up and walked over to the thick tree trunk so she could see him more clearly.

Their eyes met across the space and soon he was striding confidently towards her, his very presence commanding attention.

Angelina's eyes followed his every step, captivated by the magnetism that seemed to emanate from him. Her pulse quickened, and a delicate blush graced her cheeks as he drew nearer. She had dreamed about him so often and now he was here, it was a little overwhelming.

The distance between them closed, until he stood only a few paces away. His eyes, a mesmerizing shade of deep brown, met hers.

"Lady Angelina," He greeted her, "What a pleasure it is to see you."

"Lord Sinclair, how lovely of you to visit. I wasn't told to expect you."

He smiled, "No, it was a last minute decision. How have you been since you returned home? Have you kept out of trouble?"

A blush deepened on Lady Angelina's cheeks. "Of course!"

He gave a low laugh, "I do hope so."

Angelina found herself torn between her desire to confront him about Lady Edwina and her fear of further heartache. But she needed to hear the truth.

"My lord, I need to ask you something. I encountered Lady Edwina last week and she told me that she is engaged to be married. Is this true?"

Lord Sinclair nodded. "Indeed she is. Why do you ask?"

"She told me that she is engaged to you." Angelina watched him carefully to see how he would react.

His eyes widened in surprise, his features etched with disbelief. "Me?"

Angelina nodded. "She even showed me the ring you gave her."

He shook his head, "I never gave her anything, let alone a ring and I can assure you, Lady Edwina's words were nothing but lies. I am not engaged to her, nor do I have any intention of being." He crossed his arms over his chest. "I have no idea why she told you that. I can only assume she meant to cause you distress. I think she is of the persuasion that if she can't have something, then no one else can."

A wave of relief washed over her as she processed his words. "So she lied merely to deceive me!"

Lord Sinclair's expression softened, "She is currently engaged to Lord Archie and to be truthful, I am quite delighted."

Angelina clapped a hand to her mouth and gasped, "Lord Archie?!"

He nodded. "Maybe that little scenario you engineered was the push they needed to discover each other's true feelings."

"So I am a matchmaker!" She exclaimed and then eyeing him mischievously, she said, "In which case you shouldn't have punished me!"

Lord Sinclair pointed his finger at her. "Lady Angelina, you thoroughly deserved that punishment and well you know it."

His words set her heart racing and looking into his eyes, she saw a deep desire, one that she returned wholeheartedly. In that moment, Angelina felt a glimmer of warmth and trust rekindle within her. The truth had been unveiled, and with it, the possibility of a future that she had once believed lost.

Lord Sinclair looked at the little madam before him and decided to reveal the reason he was there.

"I wish to speak plainly, Lady Angelina. In all truth, I have been trying to distance myself from you but I find I cannot."

She went to speak and he raised his hand. "Please let me finish. If I don't say it now I never will." He looked at her intently. "I find that I cannot stop thinking about you. You have touched my heart in ways I never thought possible. So I need to ask if you would consent to becoming my wife?"

He watched her face light up and felt an immense sense of relief. It gave him the courage to continue. "I know I am a lot older than you. Thirteen years is a big gap. But you would benefit from my knowledge and I would ensure you receive every comfort you desire."

He took her small hand in his, "I have fallen in love with you. Your presence brings light to my days, and I cannot imagine a future without you by my side."

He watched as Lady Angelina's eyes shone with happiness. "Oh, I can't believe it! I have missed you so much since I returned home and now you're here and... oh!"

Without hesitation she threw herself against his chest and he quickly enfolded her in his strong arms. "My dear, I have wanted to do this for so long I cannot tell you. I never dared to assume you would feel the same. That's why I stayed away. I thought over the last few weeks I would be able to forget about you but I couldn't."

Gently, Lord Sinclair drew her away, his gaze locked with hers, searching for confirmation. "But are you certain? Are you absolutely sure that you want to marry me?"

A bright smile graced Lady Angelina's lips as she spoke with unwavering certainty. "I have never desired anything more fervently in my entire life!" she declared.

"Then," Lord Sinclair declared, a sense of purpose resonating in his voice, "let us make our way inside and seek your father's blessing."

A gentle breeze rustled through the treetops as Lord Sinclair and Lady Angelina strolled side by side across the lavish estate grounds to speak with Lord Beaumont. Both of them hoping he would find no reason to decline their wishes!

The past couple of weeks had not been easy but now, hands clasped in comfort, all felt at peace. Lady Edwina's attempt to part them had failed and Angelina couldn't be happier!

—⁀⊙⁀—

A *month later*

In the quaint chapel nestled on Lord Sinclair's estate, Lady Angelina and Lord Sinclair stood before their closest friends and family, and lovingly exchanged their wedding vows.

As the vows were exchanged, Angelina's heart overflowed with happiness. The weight of past pain had been replaced with the promise of a future filled with happiness and unwavering devotion. The words spoken echoed through the chapel, sealing their union and binding their love together.

With the exchange of rings, they became husband and wife, their love celebrated by the cheers and well wishes of their loved ones. Her mother had tears in her eyes and Susannah was smiling happily.

The chapel doors swung open, revealing a sunlit garden where the reception awaited, adorned with vibrant flowers and the melodies of laughter and merriment. Lord Sinclair's staff had worked hard to make everything perfect. The tables had been decorated beautifully with no expense spared.

She spied Amy near one of the tables and she sent her a little wave. Amy had been so happy to hear that Angelina was to become Lord Sinclair's bride and she would now serve her as her personal maid. Their connection was more friendship than anything and Angelina was looking forward to spending time with her.

The guests began to mingle and dance, the air filled with the joyful celebration. Lady Angelina and Lord Sinclair, hand in hand, shared their first dance as husband and wife, their eyes locked in a tender embrace. The world around them faded into the background as they revelled in the blissful moment of togetherness.

Much later, Lord Sinclair made their excuses and Angelina found herself alone at last with her new husband in their chambers. The bedroom was adorned with delicate silk drapes, casting a romantic glow upon the scene. Her eyes met his, mirroring the deep affection and desire that burned within their souls.

Angelina's eyes darted to the bed whilst they spoke and a blush stole over her cheeks. Soon she would experience what it was like to lose her virginity and truly become a married woman.

She heard the door close and looked over to find Lord Sinclair staring at her. Her breathing quickened when she saw the look in his eyes and mesmerised she watched him approach.

Raising his hand he touched her face, tracing the outline of her slender jaw with his fingers. She shivered with desire and her lips parted softly, yearning to feel him against her. Bare flesh against flesh.

He slid his fingers down her neck, brushing the back of his fingers over the exposed, soft swell of her breasts revealed above her bodice. Her eyes closed and she swayed, hungering for his touch.

She felt his hand entwine in her hair, pulling out the ornate clips and letting her blonde locks cascade down her back.

His strong arms wrapped around her and his lips claimed hers, gently at first, seeking her response which she readily gave. His kiss deepened, his tongue fencing with hers. She reached up and placed her hands around the back of his neck, her body aching for him, every nerve tingling with anticipation.

He moved his lips downwards, lightly kissing her neck and shoulders whilst his hands made light work of her corset, unlacing it with ease and shrugging her wedding dress from her slender body.

She stepped out of the material as it pooled at her feet and raised her arms whilst he removed her shift.

Completely naked, he lifted her in his arms and placed her on the bed, his eyes never leaving hers as he quickly disrobed. Inquisitive, she let her eyes wander over his powerful frame as each piece of clothing was thrown aside. His chest was broad and muscular, his arms thick and strong. Her eyes moved lower and then widened at the sight of his manhood. It seemed awfully large!

He noticed her look of trepidation and quickly joined her on the bed, cradling her in his strong arms. "Don't worry, my sweet Angelina. I will be as gentle as I can."

His mouth claimed hers and she lost all further thought as he skilfully began to bring her pleasure. His lips moved down her body, kissing her silky soft skin until he reached her womanhood. Cupping her bottom, he lightly flicked his tongue over her sensitive flesh, sliding over the delicate folds and her little nub of desire until she thought she could take no more. It was exquisite. Her hands gripped the covers tightly as she felt her body climb and climb, seeking the release she craved. Suddenly, her body tensed and she cried out as her orgasm ripped through her body.

Rising up, Lord Sinclair placed his powerful thighs between hers and nudged his cock at her slick entrance. She opened her eyes and gasped when he began to push into her, his thick length stretching and filling her warm centre. She clung onto his arms with a mixture of excitement and fear but trusting him completely.

He stopped for a moment, allowing her body to adjust to his size, his firm lips covering hers and then with a powerful thrust he broke through her maidenly barrier. She whimpered softly but the pain lasted only a moment before she felt her body begin to soar once more.

He moved his hips in a steady rhythm, sliding in and out of her feminine core with ease. Angelina had never known such pleasure. She shifted beneath him and naturally began to move her hips in time with his. Soon she became lost in the throes of passion, a rapturous look on her face when her world erupted again in a myriad of stars.

She felt his body tense soon after and with a deep shudder he climaxed, allowing himself the pleasure of release. He rolled onto his side and held her tenderly against his chest while their breathing returned to normal. Running his hand over the curve of her hip he asked softly, "Did I hurt you?"

She shook her head. "There was a little pain but it was soon gone."

"It will be more pleasurable next time, my love. The first can be a little overwhelming."

She snuggled against him, idly running her fingers over his chest. It felt so right to be in his arms, safe and secure from the outside world. Just him and her.

He reached down and drew the tangled sheets and coverlet over them before kissing her softly. "You are everything I ever dreamed my wife could be, my dearest Angelina."

In the quiet hours of the morning, Angelina lay satiated in Lord Sinclair's arms, basking in the afterglow of their lovemaking. Her heart was filled with a profound sense of contentment.

Who would have believed that she would marry such a man?

As the sun rose, casting a soft golden glow upon their entwined bodies, Lady Angelina snuggled into Lord Sinclair's strong arms, knowing that whatever challenges they would face in the future, she had his undying love and protection.

It was where she belonged.

The End

About the Author

Maryse Dawson was born in England but now lives in western France with her family - a husband, three children and two cats. When she's not writing she spends her time visiting the beaches and surrounding countryside. She has always enjoyed reading romances and loves history so began writing a few years ago to include domestic discipline in her stories. An alpha male - a feisty woman and adventures that will keep you turning the pages!

Read more at https://www.facebook.com/maryse.dawson.5.

www.ingramcontent.com/pod-product-compliance
Lightning Source LLC
Chambersburg PA
CBHW020600160726
47991CB00002B/802